12   B

D1533143

Copyright Notice:

This story is a work of fiction. Names, characters, places and incidents are either the product of the author's imagination or used fictitiously. Any resemblance to actual persons, living or dead, businesses, events or locales is entirely coincidental.

License Notes:

This book is licensed for your personal enjoyment only. This book may not be re-sold or given away to other people. If you would like to share this book with another person, please purchase an additional copy for each recipient. If you are reading this book and did not purchase it, or it was not purchased for your use only, then please return to your retailer and buy a copy for yourself. Thank you for respecting the hard work of this author.

Artwork: Designs by Dana

Publisher: Paper Gold Publishing

© 2020

Everything to Lose

E.M. DENNING

CHAPTER 1

ZANE

Zane grabbed three beers out of the cooler and passed two off to his kid brother, Jonathan. Jonathan passed one over to his best friend, Dante, and they cracked them open. It didn't matter that Jonathan and Dante weren't old enough to legally drink, no one around them cared. There was a bonfire, a lake, and a group of people all college bound soon.

Zane would be starting his senior year, but Jonathan and Dante were freshman. Because Jonathan wanted a career in art, he was off to some fancy art school in Los Angeles, and Dante planned to attend the same school Zane went to, a few hours away in upstate New York.

"I can't believe you're leaving tomorrow," Dante frowned into his beer and Jonathan threw an arm around him.

"You'll be fine without me."

Dante shrugged. "It's going to be weird."

"Life is weird, Dante." Jonathan tapped their beer cans together. "Drink up. The night is young and so are we." Jonathan flashed Dante one of his toothy grins and downed the rest of his beer. "Speaking of, which, I see Laina over there."

Zane watched Jonathan pat his back pocket, probably

looking for a condom, knowing Jonathan. He leaned close to Dante and breathed in his face.

"How's my breath?"

Dante stepped back and frowned. He waved a hand between them. "Fucking gross."

Jonathan shrugged. "Nothing I can do about that now. Wish me luck. Zane, watch Dante for me. Make sure if someone comes to take advantage of him, they wear a condom first." Jonathan winked and disappeared into the shadows.

"Fucker." Dante swore quietly and sipped at his beer. Dante, quieter and more reserved than his best friend, the total opposite of Jonathan, Zane sometimes wondered how the two of them could be friends. But Dante had always been a fixture in their life. He'd met Jonathan in the first grade and had been around ever since.

"He's an idiot."

Dante looked up at him. "You don't have to hang around if you don't want to. I know you probably have friends here somewhere."

Zane bumped his shoulder into Dante's. "I don't mind hanging with you." It wasn't a lie. He hadn't planned to attend the end of the summer party this year, but Jonathan begged him to go, claiming that he'd be too drunk to find his way back to the road to meet their ride.

Dante went quiet and they stood there for a few minutes watching the bonfire kick sparks up into the sky.

"Can I ask you a stupid question?"

"Shoot," Zane sipped his beer. "Jonathan does all the time."

"What's college like?"

"You nervous?" Zane glanced at Dante. The kid had his can of beer in a death grip.

"Me, nervous?" Dante scoffed and they both laughed. Shy and timid, it had shocked Zane when he'd come out of the closet. Not because it surprised Zane that Dante was gay, but it took balls to be honest about yourself and he was always so guarded.

"It's not as bad as whatever you're dreaming up in your head."

Dante snorted. "I believe that."

Zane remembered his first week on campus. He'd bounced between elated and scared shitless so often he probably had brain damage. "It's wild. You'll get used to it though. You got used to Jonathan, didn't you?"

"I had a lifetime to get used to the little shit," Dante laughed. "Did he ever tell you how we became friends?"

"Knowing Jonathan, he probably took one look at you and declared you to be his new best friend."

"I was in the sandbox and Lucy St James took my Hot Wheels. He got pissed off when she wouldn't give it back. At lunch he used to trade his pudding for her granola bar, but that day he told her he didn't want to trade anymore because she was mean to me. Then he declared me to be his best friend."

Dante was a better friend than Jonathan deserved. Jonathan was off in the woods with Laina Graves instead of here with his friend on their last night together. Dante didn't seem to mind, though, so Zane tried not to.

"College will be fine. You might not meet a Jonathan, but most of the people on campus are pretty great. You'll find where you fit."

Dante shrugged. "I suppose." He drained his beer and tossed the empty on the ground near the cooler. "I'm glad you came, by the way."

Zane grinned at Dante. "Yeah?"

"Yeah. Someone will have to carry his drunk ass to the road, and it sure won't be me."

Zane tipped his head back and laughed. "He'll be fine."

"Laina brought vodka." Dante laughed when Zane groaned.

"She fucking didn't."

"Oh, she did. Her older sister bought it for her."

"He better not puke on me."

Dante laughed again. Zane reached into the cooler and handed Dante another beer. He popped it open with a shy smile and took a sip.

"Hey, Dante, haven't seen you around all summer. Where've you been hidin' at?" Corey Mathers sauntered over and tried to fling an arm around Dante's shoulders, but he ducked out of the embrace and skirted around to the other side of Zane, as if using him for a human shield.

"Been busy, Corey."

"You got time now?" Corey was drunk as fuck and had handled more balls than a soccer team, according to local gossip. Zane glanced at Dante. Even in the dim fire light, Zane could see how uncomfortable Dante was.

"Still busy, Corey," Zane said. When he slid his arm over Dante's shoulders, Dante didn't shrug out of the touch and Zane tugged him closer.

"That so?" Corey swayed on his feet a bit. "This guy bothering you, Dante?"

Dante shook his head. "No, I'm fine, Corey. Just... busy."

Corey grunted and staggered away.

"You okay?"

Dante moved away from Zane and sipped at his beer. "Yeah. He's been trying to get me to go out with him for a while, but I'm not interested. He only wants his dick sucked and somewhere along the way he decided the person doing it should be me. Thanks for helping me get rid of him."

Jonathan was wrong about his friend, Zane thought. Dante wasn't a pushover. He might be shy and quiet, but he wasn't going to go with a Corey just because someone paid attention to him.

"Any time, Dante."

Two hours and the rest of a case of beer later, Jonathan stumbled over to Zane and Dante. He had twigs in his hair, the knees of his jeans were torn, and his front was covered in dirt.

"Have fun?" Dante asked, clearly amused.

"I fell down a hill," Jonathan laughed. "Slid all the way down like... like something that slides. You know. Those... those snow things." Jonathan held his hand flat and made a whooshing noise as he sliced through the air.

"Sleds." Zane offered, he stood and piled the empties into the cooler. "Let's head for the road. When we're closer we can text for our ride."

"Did you save me a beer?" Jonathan swayed.

"Fuck no, you gremlin. Get moving. If I've gotta carry you, I'll kick your ass."

"Brotherly love." Jonathan shook his head, but almost fell over. Dante caught him in his arms, and he watched him sway and almost go down too. No wonder he'd wanted Zane to be here. Dante was only five foot six. Jonathan was six foot, like Zane. It would've been hell for Dante to haul Jonathan's drunk ass up the trail.

"The only thing I feel for you right now is obligatory tolerance. Get off Dante before you crush him and get your ass moving."

"Get off Dante." Jonathan snorted. "I heard Corey tried to get off on Dante. Did Dante get off?"

"Shut up or I'll drop you," Dante ground out.

"No. Don't drop me. I already fell down a hill. I got lost. I lost a shoe. I found a shoe. And I held Laina's hair back. I think she threw up on my shoe. Anyway. Don't drop me. I won't get up."

Dante groaned. "You stink. I think you fell in something. Get off me."

Zane rolled his eyes. The last thing he wanted to do was carry his drunk brother to the road, but Jonathan could barely stand, and Dante looked like he was about to be flattened.

"Here, I'll trade you." Zane set the cooler down in front of Dante, then grabbed Jonathan's arm and tossed it over his shoulder. He wound his arm around Jonathan's waist, and they started for the road. "Fuck me, you reek."

"Must've been some sorta shit on that hill."

"No one will want you in their car, man." Zane tried to breathe through his mouth, but the stench was so bad he could almost taste it.

"I'll text your mom," Dante said. "I'll have her bring some clothes and a trash bag. Jonathan can change before he gets in the car."

"It's two in the morning. Mom's gonna be soooo pissed at me," Jonathan whined. "I hate it when she's mad at me."

"She'll be fine. It'll give her one final chance to mother you before you go off to college." Zane said.

Getting Jonathan to the road was easier said than done. Zane called their mom and she met them at the trailhead. She waited with three bottles of water, fresh clothes for Jonathan, and a trash bag.

"You boys have fun?" She was still in her pajamas, her long hair piled on top of her head in a messy bun. It was nearly three in the morning and she probably wouldn't go back to sleep, but Zane knew there was nowhere else she'd rather be.

"Oh Dante," She took a step back. "You can't wear that shirt in the car. Jonathan got shit all over you."

"I thought it was him I smelled."

Zane popped the car door open and rooted around in the back seat. He'd borrowed the car a few days ago when he was having work done on his and he'd left his hoodie in the back seat. He pulled it out and passed it over to Dante.

"Here. You can wear this."

"Thanks, Zane." Dante pulled his shirt off carefully and dropped it into the bag with a frown. "I don't want that shirt back."

"Oh, you thought I'd wash this crap?" Zane's mom laughed. "If Jonathan feels a strong attachment to any of this stuff, he can clean it. You boys don't pay me enough."

"We don't pay you anything, Ma." Jonathan laughed as he struggled to pop his shoes off to change his pants.

"My point exactly. Zane, can you help him before we're here all night? Sit his drunk ass in the front seat, it'll be easier for him to get out if he has to puke." She left Dante holding the bag and she climbed back into the car.

Zane looked at his drunk brother and sighed. He glanced at Dante. "Well, let's do this."

Dante nodded somberly and they both watched Jonathan fumble with his zipper. "You undo his pants. He's your brother."

Zane was going to kill Jonathan.

CHAPTER 2

DANTE

Dante stared at his dorm room and blinked. His roommate had already settled in and had set up his half of the room. A baseball uniform hung off the back of the desk chair. If he was in with someone from the team which meant lots of baseball practice and a gloriously empty room to study in.

Dante spent a couple hours making his room look comfortable. He put his clothes away and made his bed. He'd worry about decorations later. If ever. His stomach growled and he realized he'd missed dinner by an hour. He pocketed his keys and headed out to explore the campus.

It felt strange to know that Zane was somewhere in the city and he was the only person here Dante knew. He wandered down to a cafe off campus and opted for nachos and a chocolate milkshake. The summer heat still clung to the city and Dante sat in the shaded section of the patio.

He pulled out his phone and scrolled through his messages. Jonathan had sent him ten thousand selfies over the past week. He loved California and part of Dante wished he'd been interested in art the way Jonathan was. Up until a few years ago he imagined they'd have this whole great college experience together, but Jonathan had crushed that. Dante had held his disappointment back for Jonathan's sake, but even now it sometimes felt like a bitter pill.

"First day on campus and he's already found the best off campus shakes and is scowling at his phone like a true college man." Zane plopped down on the chair across from Dante and swiped his milkshake.

"Hey, Zane. What are you doing here?"

"I had to drop a friend off on campus and saw you sitting here. Thought I'd say hi. So... what do you think? What's your roommate like? What dorm are you in? Give me all the details." Zane put his milkshake back but took a nacho. "Sorry, I'm starved."

Dante pushed the plate to the middle of the table but kept a possessive hand on his milkshake. "I think he plays baseball. I saw a uniform."

"If he gives you trouble, you tell me."

Dante rolled his eyes. "I'll be fine. Not every jock is a flaming abusive homophobe. Don't be so judgy. Anyway. I'm in the Cavell building."

"Ah, good old Cave Hell. If you sneak up to the roof, make sure you block the door because it locks automatically."

"Is that rumor or experience?"

"And don't get caught. Campus security doesn't like kids on rooftops." Zane stole another nacho and moaned. "What are you doing later?"

Dante shrugged. "I have orientation tomorrow, but nothing until then. I thought I'd eat, then give myself a tour."

"I'll show you around if you want. What classes do you have? We can map out the best route for you."

Dante pulled his class schedule up on his phone and gave it to Zane. "It's all a bunch of beginner shit. You hear from Jonathan lately?"

"Nah. He has to keep in touch with mom and dad though or mom threatened to send you his share of the treats."

Dante blinked at Zane, confused.

"You didn't think you would go off to college and get away from my mom, did you? Shit, Dante, she practically adopted you. She told Jonathan to be on his best behavior or you get all his care package crap."

"That's brutal. I approve." Dante snacked on the nachos and watched Zane scroll through his schedule.

"You got all the good professors." Zane returned his phone and tried to snatch Dante's drink, but he moved it out of reach. "When we're done here, I'll show you around if you want."

"Not like I have anything better to do."

"Would you ditch me if you had a better offer?"

"In a heartbeat," Dante smiled.

Zane clutched his chest. "You wound me."

"You'll live."

"You are so cold."

"Not as cold as this delicious milkshake." Dante put the straw between his lips and took a long drink. When he pulled the straw out of his mouth he sighed. "Ah, so good."

"Pure evil."

The fun exchange between him and Zane released the tension in Dante's shoulders. The whole day had been one big change. His life had been packed up into the back of a moving truck and hauled four hours away, then loaded up into a small strange room. He didn't know how he was supposed to do the whole college thing all by himself, but with Zane around, even if only once in a while, lifted Dante's spirits.

They finished the nachos together then walked back to campus. "What room are you in?"

"Four-twenty."

"For a kid who doesn't smoke weed, that's pretty funny."

"Who says I don't?"

Zane laughed. "I'm not dignifying that with an answer. Come on. I'll show you the gym and the cafeteria."

"Not sure I need to know where the gym is."

"What? You're not going to be my spotter?"

Dante tossed his empty milkshake into a nearby trash can. The idea of being in a gym and having permission to basically ogle Zane wasn't unappealing. Zane had always been hot. He'd never admit it to Jonathan, but Zane had been his sexual awakening. He couldn't remember the exact moment it happened, but a series of events had led him to the realization that while Jonathan had a huge thing for Julie Steines, he had those same thoughts about Zane.

His crush never totally went away, but he'd long grown out of the awkwardness of it. Now his feelings for Zane were more of a warm appreciation for Zane's existence. Sure, Dante thought he was stupid fucking hot, but he was also straight. Even if he wasn't, he didn't know if Jonathan would approve of Dante's crush. It was something they'd never discussed. Even though Jonathan was the first person Dante came out to, there were things you didn't tell your best friend.

Near the gym, Zane was spotted by one of his friends. Zane introduced him as G, but G punched Zane in the arm.

"Will you fuck off with that?" He offered his hand to Dante to shake. "I'm Gomez."

"Gomez?" Dante raised an eyebrow.

"You're such a shit," Zane laughed. "His name is Ricky."

"How did you get from Gomez to Ricky?" Dante asked. He immediately flushed. His mouth tended to run away with him when he was relaxed, and Zane's presence had put him at ease.

Ricky laughed. "A Halloween costume that is still haunting me." Dante was sure there was a hell of a story there, but before he could wonder too much about it, Ricky spoke again. "What are you guys up to?"

"I'm showing Dante around campus. His orientation is tomorrow."

Dante was sure Zane didn't have to specify that. There was no way Dante looked like anything but a freshman.

"How do you know the freshy?"

"He's Jonathan's friend."

"Oh, cool. Nice to meet you Dante. Maybe Zane will bring you to one of our parties."

Dante wasn't sure if he'd fit in at a college party. Hell, he didn't fit in at the party at the lake back home. The only person besides Zane and Jonathan who had talked to him had been Corey.

"We'll see," Dante replied. He stuffed his hands in his pockets and watched Ricky and Zane talk for a few more minutes.

"I've gotta get going. I need to hit the showers."

"Hot date?" Zane asked.

"Always." He clapped Zane on the shoulder and nodded at Dante. "Nice meeting you."

Zane watched him go, then turned toward Dante. "Come on. I'll show you the cafeteria and the library. All the good stuff."

Dante's stomach rumbled. Zane looked at him. "Sorry," Dante said. "Someone ate most of my nachos."

"Okay, cafeteria, library, then I'll show you the best burger place within walking distance."

"Don't you have a car?" Dante whined. It had been the longest day of his life and though he knew he'd sleep like shit, he wanted to lay down in his dorm and not move for at least twelve hours.

"That would kill the broke college kid experience."

"If you're broke, I could lend you gas money."

Zane shot him a wry smile. "I'm fine. Thanks anyway, you little shit. Like I'd take your money anyway."

"What, my nachos are good enough for you, but my money isn't?"

"That's right." Zane ruffled Dante's hair.

Dante frowned and raked his fingers through his hair to tame the mess Zane had made of it. He tried to mind that Zane had ruined his hair, but he couldn't, not when Zane was being so nice to him.

"You don't have to hang out with me, you know. I know you're busy and shit."

"I don't mind. I had nothing going on anyway."

Dante nodded and followed Zane to the library. The building was a three-story brick monstrosity. A set of stone steps led to a huge double door. A wheelchair ramp stretched up the side of the building. "This place is huge."

"Just wait." Zane pulled the door open and ushered Dante inside.

Books stretched up toward the ceiling on shelves taller than Dante. Taller than Dante standing on Zane's shoulders. The library was freakishly huge. He'd seen pictures online, but it was even more impressive in person. "Now I know how Belle felt."

"Are you calling me a beast?"

"Are you giving me the library?"

"No."

"Then no."

"Well, that kind of sucks. I liked the beast. He was bad ass."

"I didn't know you were a fan of Beauty and the Beast."

"Don't pretend like you buy into the macho, real men can't watch cartoons, bullshit."

"That's not it. I had you pegged for a little mermaid, man, that's all."

"Nah. Not my style. Belle got to know Beast before she fell in love. Ariel was a horny teenage girl in the throes of rebellion."

"Belle probably had Stockholm Syndrome."

Zane shrugged. "Maybe, maybe not. Some people make that argument. But the beast let her go and she chose to go back to help him. I'm sure it goes down differently in the original fairy tale. It's probably way more grisly."

Zane led him through the ground floor of the library, then back outside. The sun had dipped in the sky washed the world in golden light. Zane glowed and Dante's heart raced.

It wasn't his crush coming back. He felt vulnerable in a new city and he felt grateful for Zane's company. That was it. That was all there was to it. It didn't matter that Zane was gorgeous as fuck and had only gotten hotter with age. He was Jonathan's brother. Jonathan's straight brother. Dante would not crush on a straight guy.

"I'll meet you for breakfast and show you the cafeteria before orientation. Right now, it's burger time."

"Didn't you just finish my nachos?"

"I'm a growing boy." Zane went down the stairs ahead of Dante. His ass was round and perfect under his tight jeans.

Dante blinked and dropped his gaze to the ground before he made a fool out of himself. On the list of shit that never happened, checking out Zane's ass was at the very top.

"Don't worry. Dinner's on me," Zane said.

He must have thought Dante was nervous about his cash flow, and though that was the last thing on his mind, he let Zane believe it.

CHAPTER 3

ZANE

Seeing Dante around Ricky reminded Zane of how shy he could get sometimes. The longer he'd let Ricky ramble, the quieter Dante became. In real time, he watched Dante retreat into his shell. It wasn't something he'd been used to seeing. Dante was used to Zane, and when he was around him Dante had a charmingly sunny personality.

Watching him shrivel had brought out this insane urge to protect Dante. To shield him from... from what? Discomfort? He could have driven them to the restaurant. He told himself that Dante would have an easier time finding it again if he walked it, but truth be told, he enjoyed the company and hadn't been eager to part ways last night.

Dante, as predicted, loved the food. Zane had insisted on paying the bill, but he pretended not to notice the extra bill Dante slipped into the tip money. Zane sat perched outside of the Cavell building, waiting for Dante. He'd texted him a minute ago and Dante promised to be right down.

A text from Jonathan had come through earlier that morning, asking him, again, to look out for Dante. Zane wanted to remind Jonathan that Dante was an adult now, he could navigate his own life. But nonetheless he agreed to check in on Dante from time to time.

The door swung open and Dante appeared in a crimson hoodie, the sleeves pushed halfway up his arms, his hands were buried in his jean's pockets. He had black bags under his eyes and Zane forced a smile despite the frown that tugged at his mouth.

"Hey. Looks like you could use caffeine."

Dante grunted and fell into step beside Zane.

"Didn't sleep well?"

"New bed. New place. Roommate snores."

That made Zane frown. "How bad?"

"I'd rather have a room beside train tracks. It would be quieter. Or maybe under an airport flight path. Planes landing make less noise."

"Is he nice at least?"

"Seems like a decent guy. Brant? Brantley? Something like that. I couldn't catch his name with his girlfriend's tongue down his throat."

Zane laughed. "You'll have to find some hot boy to make out with in your room. Even the score."

Dante cringed. "I'll keep that in mind. Though I'd argue that what they were doing went beyond making out. It's a good thing you showed me where the library was. I have a feeling I'll be spending a lot of time there."

"There are worse fates."

Dante followed Zane into the cafeteria, and he showed him where to line up, where to reload your cafeteria card, and when to come to get the best selection.

"What time does your orientation start?"

"In like... fifteen minutes. It's a short walk from here. I'll make it."

Zane almost asked Dante what he was doing after, but if

Dante were going to ever get used to the place, he couldn't rely on Zane to be there all the time. Even though part of him wanted to be. He remembered how lonely and weird his first week or two there had been.

"You have my number. Text me whenever you want to hang out." They stood and cleared their trays, then stepped back outside. The sky had darkened with the threat of a late summer storm.

Dante had gone quiet and Zane knew that his nerves were probably the cause. He patted Dante on the shoulder and gave it a light squeeze. "You'll be fine," he promised.

"Yeah. I'll make a hundred friends. I'll be so popular I'll have to beat the boys off with a stick."

Zane knew Dante was being sarcastic, and he grinned at him. "That's the spirit. Maybe you can borrow your roommate's bat."

"Maybe," Dante's smile was small and mostly fake, but Zane would take it. "I have to go. Thanks for showing me around and stuff."

"Anytime. And remember, if you need anything, text me."

Dante nodded, then turned and headed toward the gathering crowd of freshmen who looked as shell shocked and shit scared as Dante did. Zane forced himself to leave and not stare at Dante. He didn't need his hand held through orientation. He'd be fine on his own.

Zane shook his head. Jonathan's stupid paranoia about Dante had rubbed off on him. It didn't help that Zane knew what Dante's life had been like. As an only child in a single parent home, Dante had been left on his own a lot while his mom worked. Until Zane's mom caught on, then Dante had a standing invitation to come over every day after school and stay for dinner. Usually, Dante could be found at their house. Sometimes it was like he only went home to sleep.

When Zane returned to his place off campus, Ricky was there. He'd been roommates with Ricky all last year, and they decided to finish out their senior year as roommates again. They lived in a townhouse with their friend Noel, who was in class.

"Hey fucker. Where'd you run off to this morning?" Ricky asked. "You want a coffee?"

"I had breakfast with Dante." Zane watched Ricky pour him a coffee and he passed it over, black and sugarless, exactly how he liked it.

"That the kid from yesterday?"

"Yeah." Zane wanted to argue that he wasn't a kid, but whatever. He hoped he wouldn't call Dante a kid to his face.

"He's cute." Ricky smiled and Zane shook his head.

"Don't even think about it."

"Oh, come on, Zane. He's fucking adorable."

"Leave him alone. Let him settle in and find some kid his own age to fuck senseless." The image stirred up something in Zane's lizard brain. It protested the idea of Dante with anybody, his age or not. For reasons unknown, he didn't like the thought of Dante fucking anyone senseless.

Ricky nodded. "I see how it is." He eyed Zane with suspicion.

"What?"

"Nothing." He took a long swallow of his coffee. "Did you get the courses you need?"

"Sure fucking did."

"Down to our last year. I can't wait to be done with this place, Zane."

"Post-secondary education got you down? College life not what you thought it would be? Well, for the low-low wage of two-ninety-five an hour, you too can deliver pizzas until eternity," Zane said in his best mock-infomercial voice.

"Shut up."

"Did Noel and Vanessa talk to you about the party?"

"When they want to have it?" Vanessa was a girl Zane used to see from time to time, but strictly on a friends with benefits basis. Her friendship with Noel had always been solid and he wasn't surprised that she was in on the party planning.

"Not for a couple weeks yet."

"Do you think they're banging yet?" Ricky grinned at Zane over his coffee.

"Not my business, but I need you to help me convince them to trim the guest list."

"You don't care if they're banging?"

Zane rolled his eyes. They probably were banging, if the way they looked at each other was any indication, but Zane kept his suspicions to himself. Ricky was too nosy for his own good most of the time. "Can you focus please?"

"Fine. Fine. Sorry. But for the record, they're totally fucking. How trim do you want the guest list?"

"The last party we had was like three people away from being a fire hazard. Let's aim for considerably less people than that."

"Okay. Say we invite... five friends each?" Ricky pretended to count on his fingers. "That's... a hundred, right?"

"I will kick your ass if you let them invite a hundred people. What about close friends only?"

"Dude, that leaves the four of us."

"I'm not opposed to the idea."

"I know you're not, Mr. Anti-Social." Ricky stood and stretched. "I have to get my ass to the gym. Are you coming?"

"Sure, I got time."

Zane didn't go to the gym all that often. Usually not more than once a week, and mostly because Ricky dragged him there. He pretty much hated cardio. All forms of cardio. Especially the treadmill. The stationary bike was a close second, though.

There was nothing worse than working your ass off and getting nowhere. The whole experience made Zane vaguely angry.

"What's that look on your face for?" Ricky asked. "If you don't want to come, say so."

"I was thinking about the treadmill."

Ricky laughed and slapped Zane on the back. "You crack me up."

The gym was busy that morning and Zane wanted to leave, but he was already there and changed, so he might as well follow Ricky around. Ricky loaded up the barbell then positioned himself under it for a set of bench presses. Zane stood at the head of the bench and watched Ricky almost effortlessly blast through the first set.

He thought of his invitation to bring Dante here, and how out of place he'd be with his freshman stature and his quiet, semi-awkward nature. Speaking of semi—Zane shifted uncomfortably and refocused himself on the task of making sure Ricky didn't drop a shit ton of weight on his head.

"You're distracted today," Ricky said, dropping the bar back on the rests. He stared up at Zane. "Everything okay?"

"Yeah. I was thinking about how weird it's going to be to not be here next year."

"I will definitely only miss the freshman."

"Dude. Stop. Seriously. Do you ever think with something that's not your dick?"

"I used my brain once; I don't recommend it." Ricky grasped the bar and started another set. "Seriously, though. You need to get laid. When was the last time you went out with someone? Carley? That was like eight months ago. Have you seen any action besides your hand since then?"

"Nine months ago." Zane wasn't in a rush to find someone else to fuck. Sure, sex was amazing, but he only enjoyed sex when it was with someone he felt a connection to. Sex with strangers left him feeling weird and empty. It was an experience he hadn't cared to repeat.

"See what I mean. You need to get back out there."

"I'll think about it. There's a lot going on this year. I might not have time."

Ricky rolled his eyes. "Uh huh. Whatever you say."

"What about you?"

"What about me?"

"See anyone you like?"

"You mean besides that snack of a freshy you won't let me near? Yeah, there's a few people. There was this guy on a skateboard yesterday, total thirst trap. And there's a new barista at that place with the great cinnamon rolls. Struck out with her though. You should give it a shot. She'd probably like you."

"What makes you say that?"

"Because that's my luck. Chicks dig you because you look broody and unobtainable."

"I am not."

"Five bucks says if you go and buy a coffee from that barista, she'll flirt up a fucking storm with you."

"Come on, let's get through this torture you have planned for us. I'm already tired of being here and I haven't lifted anything yet."

"You're no fun. I need a new gym buddy."

"Deal." Zane pretended to walk away, which made Ricky laugh.

"No, wait, come back. Don't leave me," Ricky called out, a little too loud and half the gym turned to look.

"You're an asshole." Zane returned to the bench and Ricky grinned up at him.

"I know."

CHAPTER 4

DANTE

Upon finding the last textbook he needed, Dante found the back of the line and waited. Maybe he should have been proactive and started his reading over the summer like other people, but Dante wanted to enjoy those last weeks of freedom.

"Can you believe the prices of these things?" Someone said. Dante turned to see a freshman he met at orientation the other day. They'd chatted a bit during the tour the other day. Well, Linden had chatted. Dante had nodded a lot and offered the occasional, *oh yeah?* Linden came from a small town and like Dante, was there alone. He held a similar stack of books. "I think I paid less for my first car than I'm shelling out for some of these."

Dante laughed. "What kind of car did you buy?"

"Some four-cylinder piece of shit. It was rust on wheels. I got more use out of it than I probably will from any of these books. Hey, we should study together. We have the same classes and shit."

"Uh, sure, yeah. That'd be great."

Linden balanced his books with one arm and dug his phone out. He passed it to Dante. "Here, text yourself."

Dante struggled to balance the books and the phone, but eventually managed without dropping anything. He returned Linden's phone to him and moved up in the line. There was only one person ahead of him now.

"I thought I'd check out the library later and get some reading in. Did you want to meet up there around three?"

The person ahead of him finished their transaction and Dante moved up to the front of the line. Linden stuck close like a shadow.

"Uh, yeah. Three is good."

Dante paid for his books and parted ways. He lugged his books back to his dorm, where, unsurprisingly, his roommate was there with his girlfriend. They weren't naked but judging from the murderous look Dante got when he walked in, they had planned on getting that way very soon.

He ignored the heated whispers between the happy couple and stacked his books on his desk. It was way too early to go to the library to meet Linden, but he wasn't about to stay here. He shoved a couple of the texts he needed to start reading into his bookbag and hurried out again.

This didn't bode well for the rest of the year, he thought as he made his way to the cafeteria. He hadn't had time to eat that morning before his class. He grabbed a banana and turkey and swiss on whole wheat and took it outside after he paid. He found himself a nice spot under a tree to sit and lowered himself onto the grass.

He set his bag next to him and ate his banana. This didn't feel like his life anymore. His life had been back home with a parent who was never around, a family he borrowed and pretended was his own. Life on campus so far had been fine. Dante frowned as he opened his sandwich.

Most people were here living their best life and Dante was doing *fine*. He bit into the sandwich and dug in his bag for his book. All things considered; it could be worse. Clearly, Dante had watched a few too many college movies because it wasn't anything like the drug filled rager often been depicted on TV.

Dante cracked the book open and started reading. He made it through the first couple chapters before the air temperature dropped. He looked up to see a bank of storm clouds moving in on the horizon. He shoved his book back in his bag and stood. He carried his trash to a can and made his way to the library. The wind started to pick up and Dante hurried down the home stretch as the sky opened and the rain started to fall.

He burst through the doors as the rain started.

"The weather here is insane sometimes."

Dante turned and saw Ricky, Zane's friend. He had a SUBJECT book in his hand. Unlike the other day outside the gym, Ricky was dressed in a pair of dark jeans and an untucked button up. The top two buttons hung open and the sleeves were rolled up past his elbows.

"It was Dante, right?"

"Yeah."

"How do you like college?"

Dante lifted a shoulder in a half-hearted shrug. "It's... college." He thought back to the amount of money he'd dropped on textbooks earlier. "It's expensive."

Ricky laughed. "Wait until the student loan payments start."

Dante cringed. "I should sit. I'm waiting for a friend."

"I have time to kill before class. Mind if I join you?"

Dante shrugged. It was a free country. Ricky could do whatever he wanted.

He walked to a table off to the side, near the windows to

watch the rain fall outside and sat down. Ricky dropped into the seat opposite him and set his book on the table.

"You don't say much, do you?"

"Not really." Dante dug his book out of his bag, then shot Linden a text letting him know he waited in the library.

"Zane tells me I talk too much. Did you know that?"

"We don't talk a lot." Dante frowned. They hadn't used to talk a lot, but since he'd ran into Zane the other day, Zane had made a point to text him at least once a day. They hadn't found time to hang out again, and maybe they wouldn't. Maybe it would be like those days back when Jonathan and Dante were twelve and Zane did everything in his power to avoid them both like the plague.

"Well, he did. Apparently, I talk too much for my own good. My mouth gets me in a lot of trouble."

It didn't seem like Ricky minded being in trouble.

Dante's phone buzzed and he looked at the text that came through. Speak of the devil, it was from Zane. He opened the message and saw a picture of Zane looking like a drowned rat. His dark hair was plastered to his face and his shirt soaked through. Droplets of water ran down his cheeks, but despite the state of him, he smiled.

"Ooh. Someone got good news."

Dante's gaze snapped up to Ricky, who leaned over and glanced at Dante's screen. He turned his phone away, but he was certain Ricky had seen the picture.

"Snooping is rude," Dante grumbled.

"Don't worry. I won't tell him."

"Tell him what?" As casual as possible, Dante tucked his phone away.

"Exactly." Ricky winked at Dante and for some reason, the promise and the gesture did little to soothe Dante.

"Holy shit, it's raining kittens outside." Linden dropped

down in a chair next to Dante, appearing out of nowhere. He too was drenched. He raked his hand through his wet hair and little droplets sprayed Dante.

"Raining kittens?"

"You know, like cats and dogs. Whatever. I'm fucking drenched." Linden looked across the table and spotted Ricky. "Hi. I'm Linden."

"Ricky."

Linden looked at Dante. "You didn't say you knew any hot seniors."

Dante's face flamed.

Ricky, however, laughed. "He's a friend of a friend." Ricky's gaze raked over Linden's body. "Dante, you should bring your friend to our party."

"Party?"

"Party?"

Linden and Dante answered in unison.

Ricky waved a hand in the air. "Not a huge party. It's a small gathering. We throw a few every year at our place off campus."

"I'm so fucking in," Linden answered with a frightening amount of enthusiasm.

"I don't know."

"Come on, Dante." Linden turned to him and jutted his lower lip out into a dramatic pout. "As my new best friend, you're honor bound to bring me to awesome parties your hot friends invite you too."

"My new best friend?"

"Hey, we talked. Three times now. For someone as quiet as you, that's a record."

Ricky snorted. "What's your number, freshy? I'll leave it to you to nag this kid into coming."

Linden looked like he was about to come in his pants from

Ricky asking for his number. After they exchanged numbers, Ricky stood and gathered his textbook off the table.

"I have to head to class, but I'll see you later." Ricky shot a look to Linden. "Make sure he comes, freshy."

When Ricky was gone, Linden turned to Dante. "We are going to that party. If I have to fling myself on the floor and beg you, we are going."

Dante groaned. "Why do the extroverts always find me? You remind me of Jonathan. Hell, you'd probably like him."

"Who's Jonathan?"

"Zane's brother. My actual best friend."

"And Zane is?"

"He lives with Ricky. That's how I know him."

"Is Ricky single? He didn't look very taken, to me."

Dante chuckled and rummaged in his bag for his book. "I have no idea. I've had two conversations with him. You have his number, ask him."

"Oh, I plan to."

"Extroverts." Dante shook his head.

"Come on, if it weren't for extroverts..."

"Introverts would be happy?" Dante finished.

Linden glowered at him. "You're the worst best friend ever."

"I never pretended otherwise," Dante said, unaffected by Linden's faux pout.

"Good thing I have all year to whip you into shape."

They fell into comfortable silence as they started to read, but Dante's mind kept travelling back to the mention of the gym. He pictured Zane dripping with sweat, smiling at him. Dante shifted and tried not to let his brain go down that path, but there it was, picturing Zane half naked. Reliving the gorgeous scent he'd tried not to notice when Zane had loaned him his hoodie.

Maybe he'd never stopped crushing on Zane but had stopped noticing his crush because Zane was away at college. There was no way he could go to that party. He'd probably have to stop hanging out with Zane altogether. His gut clenched. He was definitely not okay with that idea.

Okay. Maybe he wouldn't have to cut off all contact with Zane, but there was no way in hell he could ever let Zane know about his insane little crush. Things between them would get weird. Zane's family had accepted him no questions asked when he'd come out, but Zane probably didn't want his little brother's best friend using him as spank bank material.

Dante's blood boiled and he shifted again. He would not think of Zane while jerking off. Not that jerking would happen any time soon. There was no privacy on campus, not even in his own dorm room where his roommate was probably fucking his girlfriend again.

At least that thought helped kill the boner Dante had given himself and he could finally concentrate on studying. As for Zane, Dante didn't know if he'd be able to avoid him. That would raise more suspicions than anything. Dante would have to suck it up and not be awkward around him.

He sighed. Awkward was his default. Dante was doomed.

CHAPTER 5

ZANE

"Earth to Zane." Ricky set a plate with two slices of pepperoni pizza on it next to Zane. "Have you stopped at all today?"

"Yes, mother." Zane leaned back in his chair and grabbed a slice of pizza. "I grabbed a banana around noon."

"It's eight o'clock. You're insane."

"It's senior year. I'm motivated to get through these last courses and get on with my life. Aren't you?"

Ricky made himself comfortable on Zane's bed. "I don't know man. Real life sounds too real for me. I don't mind college life. I'd stay here forever if it weren't so expensive."

"If you found a sugar daddy, you could become a career student."

"I don't think any self-respecting daddy would put up with my shit."

Zane laughed. "You're probably right about that." Before Zane could comment further, his phone rang.

"You're popular," Ricky said.

"It's Jonathan." Zane answered the call and Jonathan's

familiar face popped into the screen. "Hey, if it isn't my favorite gremlin."

"Shut up, maggot." Jonathan sneered.

"Someone's in a mood," Ricky said, laughing.

"Is that Ricky?" Jonathan asked. "If it is, tell him his mom says hi."

"You're a pain in the ass."

Jonathan stuck his tongue out at Zane.

"I talked to Dante earlier," Jonathan said. His forehead creased. "You talk to him recently?"

"I texted him earlier. Why?"

"Maybe it's the distance, but I know him Zane. There's something he's not telling me. Is he okay?"

"He seems fine to me. I've ran into him a few times since he got here." Jonathan frowned, not at all convinced. "Dude, trust me, okay."

"Will you check in on him soon?"

"You're not his mom."

Jonathan scoffed. "His mom is never around. That's why he needs us to worry about him."

"You're going to make a great parent one day, Jonathan. Your kids will of course hate the shit out of you."

"My future kids will fucking adore me. Go check on Dante."

"Do you want proof of life, too?" Zane had only been joking, but Jonathan nodded.

"Fuck yes. I want proof that I'm being a fucking moron and he's fine."

"You're a pain in the ass," Ricky offered. He pried himself off Zane's bed and leaned over so he could see Jonathan. "I saw him yesterday in the library. He'd barely missed getting rained on. It was very traumatic for him, I'm sure."

"You're a dick, Ricky," Jonathan sneered. He looked at Zane again. "How do you live with him?"

"My milkshake brings all the boys to the yard." Ricky blew Jonathan a kiss. He gave Zane's shoulder a squeeze and left him alone with his phone call.

"He's disturbed."

"He's not the one hounding someone to check on their best friend because of some sort of feeling. Have you tried asking him what he's keeping from you?"

"He said he wasn't keeping anything from me," Jonathan sounded exasperated.

"Maybe it's not your business."

"That's not possible. Everything is my business. I'm his best friend."

"What if he's getting laid? Do you think he'd want to talk about that with you?" Zane didn't like that image in his head. He didn't want to think of Dante naked and panting, his eyes hooded with desire, his cheeks as pink as his tongue.

"He's not getting laid." Jonathan rolled his eyes. "Will you please check in on him?"

"Fine." Zane's desire to relent had everything to do with getting off the phone with Jonathan and nothing to do with the images of Dante which flashed through his brain a minute earlier. "But if he does tell me something is up with him, I'm not telling you."

"What?" Jonathan looked shell shocked. He blinked at Zane as though he'd grown a second head.

"Whatever Dante and I talk about is our business. You have your own life to worry about now, Jonathan. It's nice that you're worried about him, but I don't think you need to be."

Jonathan frowned and lowered his voice to a whisper. "I'm allowed to worry about him. We're all he's got."

"I know." Zane exhaled and raked his fingers through his

hair. "Listen, Jonathan. I'll go now and I'll see if I can't get Dante to come out for a burger or something. I'll see how he is and if there's anything to worry about I'll handle it, okay? You can't do anything from California."

"That's why I worry about him, dumbass. If I could have, I'd have made him come to Cali with me so I could keep an eye on him."

"He doesn't need a keeper, Jonathan. Just a friend. Try to remember that." A commotion in the background prompted Jonathan to end the call. Zane set his phone down with a sigh. "It would be nice if Jonathan's anxiety about life extended to his own," he grumbled, but tapped out a text to Dante anyway.

Rather than burgers, Dante agreed to come out and split a plate of nachos with Zane again and they met there twenty minutes later. The night had taken on a damp chill from an incoming storm and Zane found Dante inside huddled in a table in the corner.

He slid into the seat across from him. "Hey."

"Hey." Dante glanced up at him. Dark bags stood out on his pale cheeks.

"You okay?" Zane asked. Maybe Jonathan hadn't been such a pain in the ass after all. "You look exhausted. School just started, it shouldn't be kicking your ass already."

"My roommate got home late, and then was up half the night shushing his girlfriend. They use our room as their own private sex nest."

"You could talk to your resident advisor. This is the sort of shit they're supposed to deal with."

"I'll try it." Dante nodded. "I hope you don't mind but I ordered already," Dante said when the waitress approached with an order of nachos. Zane watched the way Dante's eyes lit up at the sight of food, and he had to admit it was kind of cute. Dante looked like something the cat dragged in. Exhaustion lined his face and his hair was a wreck sticking out in all directions. But the mere sight of food had him lighting up like a Christmas tree.

The idea that Dante was cute shouldn't have made Zane pause, but it did. He'd thought of other guys as cute before, but only in a strictly aesthetically pleasing sort of way. But Dante had Zane all turned upside down because he wanted to fix his hair and tuck him in and make sure he got a proper amount of sleep. He wanted to take care of him.

If it weren't for the vision of kissing him on the cheek, maybe a little too close to the lips, he might have been able to pass the random thought off to how long he'd know Dante. He was protective, that's all. It had been the same way at the party when Corey tried to put his arm around Dante. Zane remembered the bloom of warmth in his chest when Dante had shirked Corey's attention, but not Zane's. In the dark of the night he hadn't been able to get a good look at Dante, but he'd gotten a good enough look to know that Dante had been adorable dressed in Zane's hoodie.

What the fuck was Zane even doing thinking about Dante in his hoodie? Or about the way Dante had felt next to him, the perfect fit he'd been against Zane's side.

"How's class?"

Dante shrugged. "Everything feels weird right now. Like is this even my life?" Dante grabbed a nacho and popped it in his mouth. Zane watched Dante chew. He became increasingly aware of everything Dante did. The way he pushed his hair off his forehead and strands of it fell back down in his face again. The way he licked the moisture off his lips after a long swallow of his pop.

"Want some?" Dante held the drink out to Zane. He only took it so he wouldn't look like some mindless idiot with a staring problem.

He took a sip of what turned out to be root beer and returned the drink to Dante. "The weirdness will level out and soon this will be your normal. By Christmas, being at home will be weird."

"Being at home was always weird."

"Hear from your mom?"

"Funny enough, yeah. She emails like three times a week. She's called a few times, too. Distance parenting always did suit her better."

"That's fucking sad."

"She cares. It's more than some people have. And I have you guys. I can't tell you what your family has meant to me, Zane."

"You don't have to." Zane was serious. They didn't often talk about Dante's life outside of their house, because as far as they were all concerned, Dante was part of their family.

Dante went quiet and sullen.

"Hey, you been on the roof of Cavell yet?"

Dante shook his head.

"I'll walk you back to the dorm and I'll go up with you."

"You don't have to."

"It'll be fun. I haven't been up there in a while."

Dante focused his attention back on the nachos. Going mysteriously quiet was sort of Dante's thing. Jonathan sometimes took it as a personal challenge to try and make him talk, to pull him out of his shell kicking and screaming. Zane didn't mind that he was quiet. He was used to it now, but tonight it bothered him a little. He didn't know why. It was probably Jonathan's worry wearing off on him.

"Are you ready to go?" Zane asked when the nachos had been consumed.

Dante nodded. "What's special about the roof?"

"Nothing, really." Zane stood and tossed enough money on

the table to take care of the bill. Dante frowned and dug out his own money. "Put that away, freshman. I've got you."

Dante scowled, but did as he was told.

"The roof is just a roof. There's nothing special about it. It's just one of those things I started doing." They entered the night and walked down the damp sidewalk side by side.

As Dante headed for the stairs, Zane's phone rang.

"Hold up a second." Zane pulled his phone out. "It's one of my roommates. Hey, Noel, what's up?"

"My fucking car died. Again. Can you come give me a jump?"

Zane's gaze flickered to Dante. He could tell Dante knew he was going to bail. "Where are you?"

"At work. I'm off shift and dog fucking tired. I have to get home to crash for a few hours, then be up early to study."

"Okay man. I got you. I'll be there as soon as I can." Zane ended the call and Dante's hand fell from the door handle. "Sorry Dante. Noel's piece of shit car crapped out. He needs a boost."

"It's fine," Dante said. He forced a smile. "I'm tired anyway. If I'm lucky, my roommate will be out, or too worn out to keep going."

"Talk to your resident advisor. You should be comfortable in your own dorm room."

Dante nodded. "Go help your friend. I'll see you around, Zane. Thanks for inviting me out though."

"Listen, Dante. Whatever you need, I'm here okay?"

Dante nodded and a hint of a smile tugged at his mouth. "Okay. See you around."

"See you." Zane nodded and made himself walk out of Cavell. He felt Dante's stare boring into the back of his head.

Zane thought about nothing else all the way to his car, and all the way across town to where Noel worked as a part time security guard. Dante had looked tired, and maybe a little lonely. Zane wanted to march up to Dante's room and give his roommate shit for his lack of consideration for others.

He found Noel parked at the far end of the mall parking lot. He pulled up next to him and popped the trunk, grabbing the cables out of it.

Noel intercepted them and hooked the batteries together. "This car is testing my patience."

"Get a new battery."

"Maybe I'll put a rock on the gas pedal and watch it drive off a cliff into a ravine."

"That's a little extra."

"I should be at home, in bed. I had plans, Zane. Big ones that involved an hour of sleep I won't be getting."

"You'll be fine, go start your car. Until you get a new battery, you can take my car."

"I love you." Noel hopped in his car and turned it over. Thankfully, it started. Zane removed the cables and put them back in his trunk. "You're a god among men, Zane." Noel blew him a kiss and closed his car door. He rolled the window down a crack. "I'll see you at home. Thanks for the boost, sugar."

"Any time, sweet cheeks."

Noel waved, then put the car in gear and eased out of his parking space. Zane climbed back behind the wheel and followed Noel home. When he walked in, Noel and Ricky were in the kitchen talking.

"What'd I miss?" Zane asked.

"We're finalizing the guest list," Noel said. He had a sandwich in one hand and a beer in the other and he was hell bent on consuming them as fast as possible by the look of things.

"Oh, speaking of guests, I invited two more."

"Come on man," Zane sighed. "We already extended how many people we were going to allow."

"Well, if you don't want Dante and his hot little friend to come, you can always say no."

"You invited Dante?" Zane furrowed his brow. "When did you do that?"

"I ran into him in the library the other day. We were stranded there because of the rain. We talked a bit and I invited him and his friend to the party."

"What friend?" Dante hadn't mentioned a friend to Zane.

"I don't know. Some hot little freshy who looked like he wanted to bang Dante, or me, or both. Maybe at the same time. I thought it couldn't hurt to invite them here."

"Goddammit, Ricky. Freshmen? Why freshmen?"

Ricky shrugged. "I'll keep an eye on them, relax."

Zane frowned. He wasn't opposed to the idea of Dante coming to the party. He'd partied with him before. But he didn't like the way Ricky had said he'd keep an eye on him. He didn't like that Dante had a hot little friend that he didn't tell Zane about. There were a lot of things he didn't like about this.

Zane cursed himself silently. "I don't mind if they come." It was mostly the truth. Zane did mind Dante coming. It wasn't that he didn't want him there, it was that Ricky had thought to invite him and Zane hadn't. "I'm going to get back to work."

"All work and no play, Zane."

"I'll play at the party."

"I bet you will," Ricky added, acting smug.

Zane slipped into his room and sat down at his computer. He stared at the screen for a few minutes. His mind wasn't on his work though. It was on Dante. His whole night had been consumed by thoughts of him and Zane, for the life of him, couldn't figure out why.

CHAPTER 6

DANTE

Without Zane, Dante had no interest in going on the roof of Cavell. He made his way to his room instead, hoping beyond hope that his roommate would be done fucking his girlfriend by now.

Dante understood wanting to fuck, not that he'd ever done it, but he could understand the urge to scratch that itch as often as possible. But he didn't know why his roommate couldn't branch out and fuck somewhere else once in a while.

Luck was on Dante's side that night. His room was empty and quiet for a change and Dante took advantage of it and slid out of his jeans then crawled into his bed. He thought he'd fall asleep right away, but he laid awake, staring at the ceiling, thinking about Zane.

Dante had talked to Jonathan earlier and right away he caught on that Dante was keeping something from him. Jonathan always could read him like a book. This wasn't a secret Dante could tell his best friend. Dante didn't want him to know the kinds of things he felt when he saw Zane. Jonathan had said on more than one occasion that Dante was family, that they were brothers. It wasn't true of course. They weren't brothers, and the way Dante's cock responded to that selfie Zane sent, it was a good thing they weren't.

Dante was lonely, not desperately so. He had Linden, who had attached himself to Dante for some reason. And he had Zane. Zane who he shouldn't crush on because he was straight. But he couldn't help it. He thought it had been something he'd gotten over, but every time he saw Zane his attraction only grew.

Dante skimmed his hand down his chest and over his briefs. His hard cock throbbed against the heat of his hand as he gripped it, unsure if he wanted to give in and stroke himself to completion or pinch it off and go to sleep.

His cock twitched under his hand, begging for a bit of action. It had been a while since Dante had even wanted to get off. He'd been too busy avoiding his roommate's sex-capades and worrying about classes and life in general that he hadn't thought about it.

Alone in the dark with Zane on his mind, Dante stroked himself through the soft jersey knit fabric of his briefs. Jacking off while thinking of Zane would be another secret added to the pile of things he'd never admit to.

It wasn't going to take long, Dante realized when he slid his hand under the elastic and pulled his cock out. His cock was hard enough to cut glass. It laid against his stomach, throbbing to his pulse. He dragged a finger up the underside, keeping his touch feather light. His thighs trembled and twitched. His cock jumped and precum leaked onto his stomach.

He bit his lip to keep his shameless moan to himself. He teased himself again, dragging his fingertips over the head of his cock. He ran his hands down either side of his cock and caressed his inner thighs, gripping them hard and arching his back. His cock twitched and throbbed, protesting the lack of attention. In his mind though, it was Zane denying him. Zane was kind, he'd probably be great in bed, too, Dante imagined. He'd want to take his time with Dante, to make sure he felt good.

Dante trembled. At this point, a stiff breeze would get him off. He wrapped his hand around his cock and jerked frantically. The fantasy of having Zane next to him, on him, touching him, wanting him, was too good to be true, but he enjoyed the burst of euphoria it brought. His hips writhed and he fucked his hand, coaxing the pleasure in his balls up to a head.

Dante moaned and shuddered as he came. He clenched his eyes shut and let himself ride out every ripple of ecstasy dancing along his nerves. Spent and sated, sort of, Dante cleaned himself up with his discarded t-shirt. He tossed it in the hamper and rolled over, intending to ride the post orgasm bliss into a good night's sleep.

He wouldn't stress about what he'd done. It was hardly the first time Dante jerked off thinking about Zane. However, it was the first time in recent years that he'd done it. It wasn't like anyone would find out. It was his secret to keep.

Thankfully, telling Zane his feelings would never be an option. He'd never have to worry about being tempted enough to make a move. His relationship with Jonathan and Zane and their family would remain intact.

Dante dropped off to sleep.

He didn't get to live out the fantasy of sleeping all night, uninterrupted, because at some time after one in the morning, his roommate returned. Dante woke to the sound of a feminine giggle, and then a shushing noise. More giggles. Moaning. Dante buried his head under his pillow and tried to go back to sleep, but his presence in the room must've been forgotten, because the two love birds didn't do anything to stay quiet.

Zane's words came back to him and Dante climbed out of bed. They didn't even notice he'd gotten up. Dante pulled on a clean shirt and a pair of cotton pants and stumbled out into the hall. He found the resident advisor's room six doors down and knocked softly.

The door swung open and a dark-haired guy blinked at him. "What's up?"

"I'm not sure of the protocol or if there's anything you can do, but I've barely been able to sleep in my own dorm room because my roommate won't stop fucking his girlfriend."

The RA nodded. "I'm Julian." He entered the hallway and closed his door behind him. "What room are you in?"

"This way." Dante turned back the way he'd come. "Sorry about waking you up, by the way."

"That's what I'm here for."

Julian waited while Dante unlocked his door and then Julian walked in and flicked the lights on. "Party's over love-birds. Unless you're going to invite your roommate to join the party, try to be a little more considerate about middle of the night fuck fests."

Dante kept his gaze averted during the commotion as they struggled to get the blankets up to cover themselves.

"What the fuck?" The girlfriend squealed.

"Put your clothes on and your boyfriend here will escort you back to your dorm. I suggest visiting the campus clinic and stocking up on free condoms. If you're going to fuck like bunnies, at least try to avoid breeding like them." Julian put his hand on Dante's shoulder. "Let's wait in the hall."

When they were in the hall and the door was shut Julian grinned. "If he gives you any shit, you come tell me, day or night."

Dante hadn't considered that, and he frowned. Anxiety swirled the contents of his stomach like a sudden snowstorm. He shivered. "Do you think he will?"

"Probably not. The campus is real strict on harassment and

stuff, and he's here on a sports scholarship. He could lose it if he gets in trouble."

Dante nodded and hoped that would be enough to keep his roommate from retaliating. Maybe Dante should've rolled over and tried to ignore it.

His roommate appeared in the hallway with his girlfriend, who glared daggers at Dante.

"Hey Brant, you should talk to Dante about his class schedule. See if you can't work out when appropriate banging hours are."

Brant nodded and wrapped an arm around the girl. "Come on Kim." It looked like she wanted to say something else, but Brant steered her away from Dante and toward the stairs.

Julian clapped Dante on the shoulder. "If they give you shit, come talk to me." Julian waited until Dante went back into his room before he left him.

Dante sat down on his bed and took a deep breath. He took a deep breath and buried his face in his hands. He hated confrontation. It made him feel shaky and off center and he hoped that Brant wouldn't want to kick his ass for what happened.

Dante climbed back into bed and tried to go back to sleep, but it was no use. He laid awake for half an hour, until Brant returned, and the light flipped on.

"You know, you could've said something to me." Brant tore his shirt off and tossed it in the laundry. "It's not like I'd care if you brought a girl back here to fuck."

Brant didn't seem angry, maybe slightly annoyed, but his lack of ire helped Dante relax.

"Sorry." He didn't have it in him to tell Brant that he'd never be fucking a girl anywhere. "I'll show you my schedule tomorrow."

Brant waved him off. "Don't worry about it. We can go to other places. The room was convenient, that's all."

"Oh. Okay," Dante said, feeling seven kinds of awkward. "Uh, goodnight then." Dante rolled over.

"Shit kid, it's not a big deal. Quit shitting your pants."

Dante let out a nervous laugh. "Sorry."

"And stop apologizing. Are you fucking Canadian or something?" The light snapped off and Dante heard blankets rustle as Brant climbed into bed.

Dante smirked. Maybe Brant wasn't a bad guy after all. He could've held a grudge because Dante had interrupted them and got his girlfriend turfed out of the dorm for the night. But he'd taken it in stride.

"Next time you have an issue with me, tell me. Okay, kid."

"Okay," he exhaled. "And it's Dante."

"Right. G'night, Dante. I have an early practice; I'll try not to wake you."

"Thanks."

The room went eerily quiet and after a moment Dante discovered that his roommate could apparently fall asleep freakishly fast. His breathing had already deepened, and a snore started to rumble out from across the room, steady and deep.

Dante didn't have the same luxury. The bit of sleep he'd gotten earlier, coupled with having to drag his ass out of bed to get Julian, and the fear that Brant would be angry with him had Dante wide awake. He looked at the time. No one would be awake to text, but he scrolled through his contacts anyway.

He scrolled back through Zane's texts and stared at the picture of him for a few minutes. He hated to admit he was disappointed that Zane had to bail before they got to check out the roof together, but he would wait and maybe Zane would offer to take him up there again one day. Maybe.

Ricky's offer to come to their party floated into his head.

Maybe Dante missed home. Maybe he clung to Zane because he was something familiar in an unfamiliar world, but Dante wanted to be around him as much as possible. Dante dropped off to sleep imagining a world in which Zane would have invited him.

CHAPTER 7

ZANE

Zane's class wrapped up and he was wrestling his laptop back into the bag when Vanessa plopped down next to him. They'd hooked up a few times over the years when they were both single and looking for a safe and friendly hook up, no strings attached.

"You busy later?" Vanessa pushed a strand of purple hair off her face.

Zane knew what she had in mind and most of the time he'd be into it, but his knee jerk reaction was to say no.

"Uh..."

Vanessa smiled. "No big deal. I haven't seen you around in a while. I thought we could catch up."

"We can have coffee or something."

Vanessa gasped and put her hand over her heart. "Talk with our clothes on? What will people think?"

Zane laughed. "Never did care much. I have time now if you wanted."

"Sure, my next class isn't for a couple hours."

Zane zipped his laptop bag and slung it over his shoulder.

Vanessa slid her arm through his and they walked out of class together.

"What have you been up to? I haven't seen you around much." She asked. Her vanilla scent wound around him. It made him think of all the times he'd been close to her. The parties she'd spent sitting on his lap. The times she texted him after a bad date. She was the sort of girl he could've fallen in love with. Only, he never did. They tried to date once, but beyond being great friends and even better fuck buddies, they didn't click on that next level.

"Besides working my ass off already this semester? Nothing."

"I hope you're still making time for a bit of fun."

"Ricky makes sure I come up for air once in a while."

They caught up on what they did over the summer while they strolled to the campus cafe. Vanessa had gone home and spent the summer riding her horse and dodging the affections of her old boyfriend.

Zane pulled the door of the cafe open and let Vanessa in first. They ordered up at the counter. Zane got an americano and Vanessa got one of her pumpkin spiced lattes. They found a table by the window to sit at. Vanessa wrapped her hands around her cup.

"So. If you're turning me down you must be seeing someone."

Zane shook his head. "Nope. Chronically single."

"I know a ton of girls who would die to go out with you."

Zane let the idea roll around in his head. He didn't hate it. He didn't love it either. Life felt too complicated lately. Too busy. He didn't know that adding dating to the mix was a good idea for him now. "Can I take a raincheck on that blind date?"

"Of course. The offer is always open."

Zane glanced over at the counter and saw Dante take a coffee from the barista. He turned for the door and their gaze met. Dante smiled. Zane smiled back and waved him over.

"Dante, come meet Vanessa."

Zane watched Dante's gaze snap over to Vanessa. He bit his lip, the way he did when he got nervous and he came over. Zane pulled the chair next to him out, but Dante didn't take it.

"I'm on my way to class but I needed a caffeine boost."

Zane let his hand linger on the back of the chair. "Dante, this is my friend Vanessa. Vanessa, this is Jonathan's friend, Dante."

"I've heard a lot about you." Dante said. "It's nice to meet you."

"You have?"

"Zane's mentioned you."

"Aww. That's sweet."

"Don't let it go to your head. I don't remember mentioning you." It was the truth. He couldn't remember telling Dante about Vanessa. But then again, it wasn't as though he kept track of every single word that came out of his mouth.

"I have to go, but it was nice to meet you." Dante barely glanced at Zane. He kept his gaze down cast. "See you around, Zane."

"Yeah. See you, Dante."

He watched Dante go, momentarily oblivious of Vanessa's continued presence.

"Oh, he's cute."

Zane looked at Vanessa but didn't know what to say to that. By all standards, Dante was attractive. But then he remembered he wasn't supposed to notice Dante that way. He said nothing to Vanessa. He didn't understand his thoughts, and as much as he'd have liked to share his inner turmoil with someone, he wasn't ready yet. He was tangled up inside. He'd sort himself out. He always did.

"You've never mentioned him before."

"He's Jonathan's friend. Hell, he's practically family." He winced at the description. It was true, but it somehow felt weird to say it like that. Like it put Dante too close to him. "He's known us a long time, is all I meant."

"He's shy, right?"

Zane nodded. "He's quiet around new people. He's coming out of his shell a little more recently. I think being away from Jonathan is forcing him to open up a little and be more social on his own. Speaking of being social, you should come to our party. It's on the weekend."

"I wouldn't dream of missing it. If you won't hook up with me, I might have to see if Noel is single."

"Don't go breaking his heart, Vanessa. He's got such a thing for you."

"I wouldn't dream of breaking Noel's heart. He's sweet."

"If you like him, why didn't you ever say so?"

Vanessa sighed and flipped her hair. "We know me. I avoid things I want and chase things that are bad for me." She winked at Zane and he laughed.

"I was never bad for you."

"You were bad for my heart," Vanessa laughed.

"I was not."

"Okay, fine. You were bad for my reputation. I was such a good girl."

Zane snorted.

"Dammit, Zane. Give me something."

"Fine. I ruined your reputation. Therefore, you should definitely not come to the party because who knows what will happen to your reputation if you're seen with me again."

"I won't be there with you. I'm going for Noel. He's denied me long enough. Are you sure you don't want me to bring a friend or two for you to meet?"

Zane shook his head. "Nah. I'm good."

"You're no fun in your old age."

"You're three weeks older than me."

"Lies." Vanessa grinned and stood from her seat. "I should go. I want to hit the library for a bit before class."

"See you later. I'll text you and remind you about the party."

"You better. Say hi to everyone for me." Vanessa bent down and pecked Zane on the cheek, then she left the cafe.

Zane stared at his coffee and took a swallow. He should get home and get some work done, but he didn't feel up to it. Maybe Vanessa should set him up with someone. His life had become a routine of school and the occasional gym session. But the thought of meeting someone with the express purpose of dating them, of going through all the motions to see if he would even be interested in them, sounded like a lot of work.

Zane wasn't jaded, he believed in love. He believed somewhere out there, there was someone for everyone. He didn't have a lot of faith that he'd meet his special someone from a blind date arranged by an old fuck buddy.

He wanted love, and love couldn't be forced. You couldn't will it into existence. You couldn't make it happen if it wasn't going to. He'd learned that with Vanessa. For as much as he cared for her, it hadn't been love. It would never be love. And he'd tried. He thought she was perfect for him. They had a lot of fun together. She was smart and compassionate, and hot. They had great sex, but something had been missing.

Blind dates might be something he'd explore down the road, but for now Zane was content to wait and see where life took him. It wasn't as though he was in a hurry to settle down. He was young and still had years ahead of him to do things like get married and start a family. Though he couldn't see himself with kids. That was more Jonathan's thing. Jonathan would be a great dad. He was a big kid himself, but he had a good head on his shoulders.

Zane made his way back home and climbed the stairs to his second-floor bedroom. He dug his laptop out of the bag and set it on his desk, then checked his phone. He was surprised to see a text from Dante.

Took your advice. Talked to the resident advisor. As a bonus I don't think my roommate is interested in murdering me in my sleep for being a cock block. Thanks.

Zane smiled at the message and typed out a reply.

That's great. I'm glad your roommate isn't going to kill you. I'd miss you.

Zane dropped down on his bed, his mind suddenly taking a dark turn. A life without Dante. He would miss him. It wasn't a lie. He hadn't missed Dante before. It had always been good to see him whenever Zane went home from college, but he couldn't remember missing him.

The way he missed him when Dante wouldn't stay for a

coffee with him and Vanessa. He hadn't noticed his disappointment in the moment, but it stung now that Dante hadn't sat
with him.

Dante had always been Jonathan's friend. Sure, over the
years they'd hung out and did things together, but Jonathan had
always been there as a buffer between them. This was the first
time in their whole life Jonathan wasn't around to fill that role
and somehow, without him, Zane's friendship with Dante had
changed.

I'd miss you too Zane

Zane stared at the text. He could feel the pinch to his eyebrows
as he read it over and over again.

**Are you sure you're not going to have an issue with
your roommate?**

Zane asked. He didn't like the idea of Dante being in trouble
and Zane not knowing about it. He wanted to protect him, even
though all signs indicated Dante could take care of himself.

I gave him my class schedule.

Dante inserted a few laugh-until-you-cry emojis.

. . .

Hey! I don't even have your schedule.

Zane didn't know what possessed him to say it, but the next minute Dante fired off a screen shot of his schedule. He stared at it, bewildered by his own behavior.

Are you going to stalk me now?

Zane laughed.

I haven't ruled it out LOL

Zane found himself smiling, his earlier moodiness had lifted. Zane forgot to worry about the future or blind dates or falling in love. He let himself enjoy his conversation with Dante.

We're having a party.

Zane sent.

You should come.

He watched the three little bubbles bounce up and down while Dante typed out his reply. And when it came through, Zane saw red.

Ricky already invited me

CHAPTER 8

DANTE

He didn't care that it came after Ricky had already invited him to the party, Dante's insides sang when the text popped up on his screen. He'd been apprehensive when Ricky had issued the invitation, and he hadn't been certain that he'd go, because if Zane didn't want him there it would get awkward. But there was no way he would miss it now.

I'll be there.

He sent before Zane could respond to his last text.

Tell me when.

Next Saturday night.

. . .

Dante's phone buzzed with a text from Jonathan.

Call me, fucker.

He texted Zane that he had to call Jonathan and was excited about the party before doing Jonathan's bidding. He answered on the first ring.

"What took you so long? I know you're not in class right now."

"I was busy. Zane wants me to go to a party he and his room-mates are having."

"My brother is popping your college party cherry. That's epic."

"I think that must be the most disturbing thing you've ever said to me." Dante reached down and adjusted his burgeoning erection. His stupid dick liked the idea of Zane popping his cherry. It still didn't care that Zane was straight and off limits. "How's school?"

"Fucking insane. I'm learning so much here. I don't think I ever want to leave. The weather is fantastic. I haven't worn socks the whole time I've been here."

"Don't be hating. Socks are amazing." Dante had started a collection of socks with fun patterns. He currently wore a pair with the Avengers on them. He wasn't into superheroes, but the socks were cute, so he bought them.

"I'll send you all my old ones if you like them that much."

"There is something seriously wrong with you," Dante deadpanned.

"Oh, buddy, there's a lot wrong with me," Jonathan laughed.

Dante mused to himself how different Jonathan and Zane were. Jonathan was loud and out there, confident in a blatantly extroverted way. Whereas Zane's confidence was quieter. Dante knew he shouldn't be lying on his bed thinking about Zane, especially not while talking to Jonathan, but he couldn't help it. His renewed crush was quickly morphing into a full-blown obsession.

"So, tell me about your school. Make any new friends? See any hotties?"

Dante ignored the part about hotties. "There's a guy named Linden who has declared himself to be my new best friend."

"We'll circle back around to that bullshit in a second. Tell me about the hotties."

"You're straight."

"That's never stopped us from talking about this shit before. I told you all about the girl in my still life with the legs that were a mile and a half long."

Dante sighed. "Fine. There's this one guy." Dante tried to think of anyone except for Zane, but he couldn't. He closed his eyes and imagined all his classes. The campus. The city. But Zane's was the only face that would materialize in his mind. "He's nice. A bit older. But he's like... tragically straight. So... it's fine. There's plenty of guys here." Dante sighed.

"That's all. Just one good looking guy?"

"I'm boring," Dante laughed. "I know."

"Hey now, none of that shit. That's my best friend you're talking about and he's anything but boring. Okay, so he's a bit quiet, but that's part of his charm. Anything exciting happen?"

Dante filled Jonathan in on when he'd gone to the resident advisor at one in the morning. He had barely seen his roommate since, which didn't break his heart at all.

"Wow, little Dante is finally growing up."

"Shut up," Dante sat up on his bed and stared at his stack of textbooks. "It's weird here without you."

"It's weird without you too, but we'll see each other at Christmas."

"Christmas? What about Thanksgiving?"

"Ah shit. I thought I told you."

"Told me what?"

"There's a huge art show here that weekend. I want to go and check it out. I've had a bunch of holidays with you, and this artist is only here for a few shows and that's the only one I can make it to."

"You suck."

"I know!" Jonathan cried. "I'm sorry."

"It's fine. I'm just giving you a hard time."

"Besides, flights add up. You're lucky you're only a few hours from home and you can catch a ride with Zane."

Dante's cheeks flushed, making him thankful that he wasn't on facetime with Jonathan. "True," Dante said.

"You don't sound very happy about that? Is he giving you a hard time?"

"Zane? Give me a hard time? No. He's been great. I'm bummed that you're not coming home until Christmas."

"I know, but it'll be here before you know it."

Dante exhaled. "I have like, a million assignments to do."

"Okay, I'll let you go. And tell the pseudo-best-friend asshole he better not turn out to be a jerk or I'll come there and kick his ass myself."

"I'm not telling him that."

"I'll have Zane deliver the message. Or maybe I'll have Zane kick his ass."

"He won't and you know it."

"Ugh. Whatever."

"You know you're irreplaceable, right?"

"Damn fucking right. I am a treasure. You're not so bad yourself though. Take it easy, Dante. Talk soon."

"Talk soon, Jonathan."

The line went dead and sounds from the real world rushed back in. The muted conversations in the hallway. The thud of footsteps and doors shutting. And the sound of his stomach grumbling.

Dante forced himself to get up off his bed and head down to the cafeteria. He grabbed a tray and went down the line filling it with food. Some juice. A Jello for dessert. He grabbed a couple slices of pepperoni pizza and sat down at an empty table.

He was halfway through his first slice when Linden plopped down across from him. He nudged Dante's foot under the table.

"Hey. What's up?"

"Nothing." Dante shrugged and cracked his apple juice open.

"Did you ever make up your mind about the party?" Linden was all wriggles and excitement like a puppy.

"Yeah. I'm going."

"And taking me?"

"And I'm taking you."

"Hell yes." Linden beamed at Dante. "I told you you're my new best friend, didn't I?"

Dante remembered the warning from Jonathan and smiled.

"What's so funny?" Linden popped a bag of chips open and stuffed one in his face.

"I talked to Jonathan today and told him you said you're my new best friend. He said if you fucked me over, he'd have Zane kick your ass."

"Is Zane hot? Because if he's hot, I'd totally let him kick my ass."

"He's not going to kick your ass."

"Shame. Because judging from the way you blushed, you think he's hot."

Dante's face went up in flames. Linden wasn't Jonathan, he could confide in Linden about his crush on Zane and not worry about ruining a decades long friendship.

"He's hot. But he's my best friend's brother. And he's super straight. He's totally hands off."

"Got it. Strictly in the jerk off *too* and not *with* category."

Dante choked. "There is something wrong with you."

Linden grinned. "I know. So... what do you plan to wear to the party?"

Dante shrugged. "I don't know. The same shit I wear every day."

Linden shook his head. "Not going to happen. I've already found this great thrift store near here. The owner is a fucking gem. Finish eating and I'll take you there."

The thrift store Linden took him to lay a short walk from campus, something Dante was starting to love about his new town. His hometown was small and spread out. Public transit sucked, for lack of a better word. If you didn't have a car, you were basically trapped.

Here, everything was in reach. A few minutes in a car or a few more on foot and you were set. If he wanted, he could get on the bus and go anywhere in the city. The sense of freedom that swelled up in him exhilarated and terrified him all at once.

Linden bumped his shoulder into Dante's. "This is it."

The building wasn't much to look at. Two stories of white plaster sandwiched between aging brick buildings. An awning in rainbow colors with the name Casual Bottoms Thrift Store caught Dante's eye, making him smile. Linden dragged Dante inside.

The guy behind the counter looked young. He couldn't be

thirty yet, if he was a day over twenty-five. Linden gave him a broad grin. "I told you I'd be back. And I brought a friend. Ansel, this is Dante. Dante, this is Ansel. We're here for party clothes."

Ansel pointed to the back of the store. "Change rooms are through the beaded curtain. Help yourself. If you're looking for something in particular, let me know if I can help."

"Thanks, Ansel." Linden led Dante to the back of the store, and they stood in the narrow aisle between the racks of clothing. Dante noticed that rather than having two sections, the styles were thrown together. Skirts and dresses hung next to pants and button ups. The whole store was color coded. Red with red, bleeding into oranges then yellows. Dante made a beeline for the blue.

Dante scanned the racks and gave a half-hearted scan. Beyond picking out cute socks, clothing wasn't his thing. He never spent much time picking out something to wear.

"Do you need help?" Linden asked. He'd already plucked a few shirts and had them draped over his arm.

"I can dress myself," Dante scoffed. A cobalt shirt in a soft, shimmery fabric caught his attention and he pulled it off the rack. The button up looked like it would fit him, and he had a pair of black skinny jeans he could wear with it. "See. Already found a winner."

Linden whistled. "Hot. That will go well with your pale ass complexion and your pretty eyes. You'll be the bell of the ball."

"Oh, shut up," Dante almost put it back, but Linden was right. It would look amazing on him. He found the tag. "It's only five bucks."

"See, I told you this place was awesome. Are you going to try it on?"

Dante shook his head. "Should I? It's my size."

Linden took the shirt from him and held it up. "Nah, it'll fit you good. I'm going to try this shit on. Come on, you can be the judge." They went behind the bead curtain and Linden set his selections down on a bench in one of the two cubicles.

Linden changed into a cream-colored sheer shirt.

"Your nipples stand out," Dante said.

"Sold." Linden peeled that one off and slid into the next shirt.

"Shouldn't you be in the change room?"

"Why? There's no one back here but us, and I'm only buying shirts." Linden ran his hand down his naked chest. "Why? Like what you see?"

Dante scoffed, but didn't confirm or deny. With thoughts of Zane on his mind every waking moment, it was hard for Dante to find anyone else attractive. But in a world without Zane, he might've liked Linden. "I guess you'll do."

"Spoken like a man who is truly fucked. You're really gone over that Zane guy, huh?"

There was no point in arguing. "Basically. It'll pass. It has before."

"Bummer, dude." Linden slid into a green shirt with white stitching.

"That one looks sharp on you."

"This is more of a date shirt." Linden pulled it off and dressed back into his old shirt. "I'll wear the nipple shirt."

"I'm shocked. Truly."

"Do you need anything else while we're here? Accessories? Underwear?"

"Okay, first off, ew. Thrift store underwear is on my never-will-I-ever list. And I'm not an accessory kind of guy."

"Not even a nice belt?" Linden shook his head. "Right, that's one more obstacle to get in the way. Good point." He clapped Dante on the shoulder. "Let's pay for this stuff. You're going to look so hot."

"Thanks," Dante said. Not that it would do him any good. Even if he could catch someone's eye, it wouldn't be Zane's. But maybe he could meet someone at the party. Someone who was available. Someone who wasn't Zane.

CHAPTER 9

ZANE

Zane popped the tab on a can of beer and took a long swallow. He'd found a nice spot of wall to lean against between the kitchen and the living room. It had a nice view of the front door, and he was only waiting on Dante to make sure he got introduced to everyone. That was the only reason.

As discreetly as possible, he wiped his clammy hand on his jeans. He'd been to parties with Dante before, so he didn't know why this one made him nervous. It could have something to do with it being Dante's first college party. He might not be legal to drink but it still made him seem more like an adult.

Somewhere along the way, Dante had grown up, Zane realized. It was hard to believe, since he'd known him since they were both kids with skinned knees and gapped teeth. Dante's presence formed the background of many of Zane's memories. That's why he wanted to look out for him.

"Waiting on your boy?"

Zane almost choked on his drink. "He's not my boy."

Ricky grinned and brought his drink to his lips. "But you knew who I was talking about."

"You need a hobby."

"Bothering you is my hobby." The doorbell rang and Ricky passed by Zane. "I'll get it."

Zane watched as Ricky sauntered over to the door and opened it. The party was tame compared to some of the frat parties and other house parties Zane had been to, but the sight of Dante walking through the threshold into his house twisted something inside him. He wanted to protect him, which was stupid, Dante didn't need a babysitter.

Zane watched as Ricky led Dante and his friend, Linden, inside. He flung an arm around Dante and leaned in close. Zane couldn't tell what he'd said, but whatever it had been it made Dante smile.

As they approached, Dante's gaze flicked up and met Zane's. Pink slashed across his cheeks for a moment before it vanished. Zane's heart responded to the way Dante looked at him with a series of flutters. Flutters in your chest should be a bad thing, it meant you were dying, or maybe dead already. But in Dante's presence Zane felt electric and unmistakably alive.

"Glad you could make it."

Dante nodded. He still hadn't shrugged Ricky's arm off him. Zane didn't want Ricky touching Dante. He didn't care what Ricky did, not ever. Or who he did. His business was his own, but the sight of his arm draped over Dante's shoulder made him angry.

"Nice place."

And there was his in. "Let me show you around." Zane motioned for Dante to walk ahead of him. He left Ricky and Linden behind, much to Linden's delight. That kid should never play poker, Zane mused as he followed Dante through to the kitchen.

Zane opened the fridge and handed Dante a beer.

"Supplying a minor. Won't you get in trouble?" Dante cracked the top open and took a drink.

"Don't get caught."

"I must say, this place isn't what I expected."

"How so?"

"Well, considering four guys live here, it's a lot cleaner than I expected."

"You're a brat." The electric butterfly sensation had calmed, and Zane exhaled a sense of relief. He didn't understand what his feelings were or when they'd changed, but Dante seemed to be the center of the upheaval inside him.

Zane had grown up a typical guy. Average at sports. Average in school. Decent human being. He liked fast cars and hot women. But now, that familiar tingle of temptation, of attraction and thirst happened when Dante got near. He lived for the way Dante smiled at him sometimes. The way his eyes would soften despite the absolute intensity of his gaze.

Zane needed fresh air. His head spun with all the things that clicked into place as this knowledge slid inside and unlocked a part of him, he'd never paid much attention to.

"Come see the back yard." Zane pushed his way through the group of people huddled near the back door. He didn't bother introducing Dante to any of them. His burgeoning discovery had him in a weird mood.

They stepped out onto the back patio. Most of the guests were in the house, but a couple had made it out to the patio chairs and were making out. Zane avoided them and took Dante out onto the back lawn. "It's not much." Besides the patio the only thing in the backyard was the barbeque and a large tree. A tire swing hung from one of the large branches.

"Did you bring me out here to swing?"

"We could if you wanted."

Dante shrugged and walked toward the tree but didn't opt to get on the swing.

"It's a nice yard."

"Nothing like back home." His parents had a huge yard and a deck with a great view of the sunset. His dad loved all things grilled or smoked. Summers were spent by the pool they'd set up, eating burgers, and soaking in the sun.

"Still nice though." Dante motioned to the patio. "Do you ever use the grill?"

"Dad would be sad if I didn't. I'm not nearly as good as he is, but I can manage not to burn things into oblivion."

"That's progress. Remember the hotdogs you tried to make that one time?"

"It was my first time barbecuing. I didn't know they'd cook so fast." Zane laughed.

"They turned to ash when you tried to get them off the grill."

"Hotdogs aren't real food anyway." Zane finished his drink. "Do you want to head back in? We can get another drink and I can finish showing you around."

"Sure. I'll probably have to peel Linden off Ricky by now. If he had things his way, they'd be touring Ricky's bed right about now."

Zane laughed. "I saw the way Linden looked at him."

"Ricky doesn't stand a chance. Linden tends to get what he wants."

They grabbed new drinks, abandoning their empty cans on the counter with a line of others. Zane introduced Dante to a few people but was greedy for him. He wanted to hoard his company.

They found Ricky and Linden in the living room. Each of them had some sort of cocktail in their hands. Linden laughed and leaned in closer to Ricky.

"Glad to see you guys are getting along," Dante said to Linden.

"Zane gave you the grand tour?" Ricky said. "Did he show you his room?"

Zane rolled his eyes. He wanted to tell Ricky to shut up, but he also did want to show Dante his room. "Not yet."

Yet was a loaded word. It came with the weight of implication, one Zane felt travel down the length of his spine and pool in his center like a hot coal. He took a drink to try and cool it.

The four of them fell into an awkward silence. "I need to take a piss. I'll be right back." Zane left the three of them standing there and vanished into the bathroom. He dumped his beer down the sink and stared at himself in the mirror.

He'd never imagined himself with a guy, but the suggestion of taking Dante up to his room put ideas into his head. Ideas he wasn't sure he was ready for. And why Dante? Dante was a friend; someone he'd known almost his whole life. And that's why it didn't matter what he felt about him. Dante wasn't someone Zane could have, especially if he wasn't sure what he felt.

He took a piss and washed his hands and when he left the bathroom, he spotted Vanessa coming down the stairs with a drink in her hand and a smile on her face. She straightened her blouse with one hand. Zane went to her. Dante was in good hands with Linden and Ricky.

"Hey, you." Zane looked at Noel who stopped at the top of the stairs. He looked down at Zane and his jaw dropped.

"Zane, buddy. Uh... shit. I can explain."

Zane shook his head. "Dude, Vanessa isn't my girlfriend. You have nothing to explain."

Noel exhaled and Vanessa reached for him as he descended the last couple of steps to her. "I told you he was fine with it."

"I know, and I trust you, but shit... bro code and all that, you know. You don't put the moves on your friend's girl."

"She's not my girl, Noel." Zane clapped him on the shoulder. Zane stood there with Noel and Vanessa and ignored the way Dante's absence felt like a betrayal. He'd invited him but had left him with Ricky. He told himself it was fine, that Dante wouldn't mind. He was there to meet people and hang out. Until Zane figured out what was going on inside his own head, he thought he should keep his distance from Dante.

That thought prompted Zane to glance through the crowd. Dante perched on the arm of a couch near Linden and Ricky and a few of Ricky's more obnoxious friends. Zane's hackles rose when someone approached Dante. The look in his eyes was pure lust and he eyed Dante like he was a snack.

He watched, frozen as the guy reached for Dante. He put his hand on Dante's shoulder and Dante blushed. His cheeks turned the same pinky hue that made Zane's heart electrify. He hated that blush. It didn't belong to some asshole who didn't even know Dante, who only saw him as a sweet piece of ass. It should be his. He knew Dante. He knew how kind he was. How caring and sweet. How funny he could be sometimes, even when he wasn't trying.

Zane's feet carried him across the room. Vanessa's inquisitive voice was lost to him. He zeroed in on Dante and approached with ire in his veins. He put a possessive hand on Dante's shoulder. "Sorry I got held up. Come on, there's something I want to show you."

Ricky snorted and Zane shot him a dirty look, but Dante stood. He shrugged at Linden, then looked at Zane.

"Lead the way."

Zane's resolve swung on a pendulum between yes and no. Dante walked close behind him, and when he paused to open his bedroom door, he could almost feel the heat radiate off Dante.

What the fuck was he doing?

Dante followed him into his room. The click of the door

latching made Zane flinch as though a gun had gone off. He turned to face Dante.

"Are you okay?" Dante asked. He leaned against the door. Zane noticed that he didn't have a drink with him anymore either.

Instead of answering Dante's question, Zane took a deep breath. "So, this is my room. It's a bit of a mess." Zane frowned at the unmade bed and the laundry scattered near the basket, instead of inside it.

"I take it you weren't expecting company up here?" Dante's voice was a whisper among the steady thump of bass that filtered through the closed door.

"Not really." Now that Zane had Dante up here, he didn't know what he was supposed to do. Bringing him up here had been a terrible idea, because for all the reasons he could think of not to, he still yearned to press him up against that door and kiss him. He wanted to see if his hair felt as soft as it looked. If he'd smell different up close. If he'd whimper when Zane dragged his lips down his throat and tasted his skin.

"Zane?"

Zane met his gaze.

"Did I do something wrong?"

"What?"

"You're... different tonight. Quiet."

"It's not anything you did, Dante."

"But something's wrong?"

"I don't know if wrong is the right word." Zane's body vibrated. He shouldn't. He fucking shouldn't think of going through with it. It could ruin so much.

A million reasons why weren't enough though, not when Dante's eyes met his and that pink blush returned to his cheeks. Then, Dante's gaze flicked down to Zane's mouth and back up again.

Zane took a step forward, then another. And for a fraction of a second, right before his lips brushed against Dante's, he paused. He could stop here, at this moment. He could pull back and blame it on the beer.

But he heard the hitch in Dante's breathing and a million reasons weren't enough to stop him.

CHAPTER 10

DANTE

The cool feeling of the door pressing against his back grounded Dante, otherwise he might not have believed what was happening. Zane was kissing him. He brushed his lips over Dante's. Once. Then again. And the third time they lingered. Zane's hands rested on Dante's hips, their stuttered indecision of pulling him closer or pushing him away highlighted how new this had to be for Zane.

And Dante didn't care that he'd given his first kiss to some now faceless guy in the eighth grade after an impromptu game of basketball one spring night. This was his first kiss. The first one that mattered. It lasted a moment. A lifetime. It felt endless but was still somehow over too soon.

Zane pulled back slowly, before they'd deepened the kiss beyond a few exploratory caresses of tongues on lips. Before Zane could let go, Dante grabbed his wrists.

"Holy shit. This is real," Dante felt high. Or drunk. Or really fucking happy.

"Dante..."

Dante didn't want to look at Zane. Whatever Zane was going to say next; Dante was sure he'd hate it and he wanted a few more moments of blissful ignorance. Because Zane was going to say he'd been drinking. That he only wanted to see what it was like. That he was lonely and made a mistake. He was going to make an excuse and send Dante away into the night, alone and broken. It would be worth it. But not yet. He wanted one more minute to take with him.

"Dante," Zane said again.

Dante lifted his gaze and said the first thing that came to mind. "I thought you were straight?"

"Surprise?" Zane furrowed his brow. He tried to pull away, but the look on his face made Dante tighten his grip on Zane's wrists. He didn't look scared or anything, but soft and vulnerable. Dante put his blossoming lust aside.

"Surprise? So, this is new? You can talk to me, you know. You're like, the second person I came out to. I get it. Whatever's going on with you, I understand." He understood more than that. He knew Zane likely only kissed him because he didn't know how to say it. Because he had this secret inside him and keeping it in sometimes felt like having a volcano in his chest.

"It's new," Zane whispered, looking down at where Dante's hand still held Zane's wrist.

"How new?" Dante's bass-drum heart pounded in his ears.

"Pretty new. I didn't... I don't... I still like girls."

"So, not gay."

"Not gay," Zane exhaled.

"Bisexual then?"

Zane opened his mouth and it looked like he wanted to say something. Then he shut it and nodded. "Bisexual." He said it almost like a question.

"You don't have to decide tonight."

Zane's shoulders relaxed and Dante took it as a sign that he would be okay. He let go of Zane's wrists, but Zane didn't move.

It wounded Dante to think that he'd been an experiment.

That Zane had felt comfortable enough with him to test the waters. He wanted to be mad but couldn't. Zane would never deliberately hurt him. There was no way he could've known about Dante's crush on him. He'd chosen Dante because he was safe. He found he didn't mind and was glad he could be there for Zane.

Dante forced himself to take a deep breath. The world hadn't stopped spinning since the moment Zane kissed him.

"Dante," Zane said with more tenderness than he should. Maybe he'd realized what he'd done. What sort of mistake he'd made. Maybe he hadn't liked it. Maybe he'd decided that he wasn't bisexual after all and this was a failed experiment. "Dante, look at me."

Dante lifted his gaze and Zane leaned in again, sealing their mouths together again. This time he kissed as though he were sure about what he was doing. About who he was kissing.

Did he understand what was going on? No. But he didn't care. He rested his hands against Zane's chest to assure himself this was real. Zane cupped Dante's face in his hands and gently explored Dante's mouth.

Dante let himself get swept away in the moment. It washed over him like a tide, sweeping him out to sea. Zane had always been a force of nature to Dante. Someone steady and dependable. Now, he was a storm, battering Dante's defenses, stripping them away with every graze of his lips.

Dante could only hear their desperate breathing, ragged and shallow, and the rush of his blood in his ears. How could any of this be real? The reality of kissing Zane was better than any fantasy he could've dreamed up. His imagination hadn't prepared him for the heat he'd feel all over. For the all-consuming urge to grind up against him, to own him and possess him in any way possible, for as long as he could. Because he knew as good as this was, and it was everything, it couldn't last.

Dante wouldn't get to keep this, and that thought spun him around and almost brought him back to his senses. Then Zane whimpered. Some small, defenseless noise from the back of his throat. Caught in the moment, Dante lived for that sound. He didn't have a lot of experience, and the knowledge someone whimpered for him, under his touch, because of his mouth, it was almost enough to kill him where he stood.

"Zane," Dante paused for breath. He spoke Zane's name with his lips still brushing against Zane's. He didn't want to stop. He never wanted to stop. He would be happy to stay in Zane's room and kiss until his dick fell off. But there were so many things Dante needed to know.

"I know." Zane exhaled. He dropped his head down onto Dante's shoulder. Because Zane stood a few inches taller than Dante, it was a bit of an awkward angle, but he made it work.

Dante leaned into Zane. He wound his arms around Zane's waist and spent a few minutes ignoring the throb between his legs and the swarm of questions in his head. Whatever would come next would probably be something neither of them liked. Because every moment they weren't kissing, Dante spent thinking about why they shouldn't be doing this. He had everything to lose.

Fuck.

What if he'd already fucked it up? Zane had kissed him, but Dante had invited it. He'd wanted it. He'd practically put a fucking billboard on his forehead.

"What are we doing?" Dante whispered in the dark. "We're insane."

When Zane laughed, his breath puffed against Dante's shirt and he wished they were in Zane's bed so he could feel it against his skin.

"I have no idea. That's... a problem, isn't it?" Zane finally straightened, but he kept his hold on Dante, as if he feared

Dante would bolt out of the room at the first opportunity. He might not even be wrong about that. Dante shook.

"Why... why did you kiss me?" Dante didn't want to spend the rest of his life wondering why. Whatever the reason, he could handle it.

"I wanted to. I... I think I've wanted to for a while."

Dante stopped breathing. "I'm sorry. What?"

Zane laughed. He sounded breathless and confused. He pulled Dante over to his bed and they sat down next to each other.

"I... I wanted to kiss you."

"We've established that." This wasn't happening. It couldn't. None of it could. "Why? Why me?" Everything was out of control. Dante forced himself to take slow, deep breaths. He had to weigh every word carefully. He had to get out of this night with his life intact. If he said the wrong thing. If he did the wrong thing, life as he knew it would be over. Zane and Jonathan, their parents, they were all Dante had. It would be easy for Zane. he'd still have his life, his support network.

Without them, Dante was lost.

"Why not you?"

"Because we're... we... Jonathan. Because Jonathan is my best friend. He's your brother." He kept the rest of his fears to himself. Zane would only invalidate them. He'd tell Dante that they could whatever they wanted, that no one would get hurt, that everything would work out fine. Nothing would change. Even if everything went sideways, he'd still have them all. But Dante knew the truth.

His mother had taught him that people only kept promises that were convenient for them to keep. She promised to love him unconditionally, then his dad left, and she stopped. She promised to be around more often, but then took more hours at work.

Zane would promise nothing would be different. Because Zane would believe it. But even now, Dante knew things had changed. There was an awareness between them that hadn't been there before. Whatever secrets they'd harbored from each other, Zane had blown them out into the open with his deliciously thoughtless kiss.

"Jonathan has nothing to do with this. You're important to me, Dante."

Dante wanted that to mean something more.

Of course, he meant something to Zane. He was Dante. He'd been around for years.

"You're important to me, too Zane." Dante took a deep breath and smothered his face in his hands.

"I'm not sorry I kissed you, Dante."

Dante made himself look up. He'd long ago memorized Zane's features. The angles of his jaw and the lines of his nose, the thickness of his eyelashes. But he'd never seen him like this. Bathed in low light, vulnerable and soft. All for him.

"I'm not sorry, either."

Zane reached for Dante, but Dante stood, throwing distance between them.

"Dante," Zane stood, but didn't move toward him.

"I don't know what to say. I don't know what to do."

Zane nodded. "This wasn't a whim. It's not a phase. I'm not going to regret this tomorrow, Dante. I won't pretend it never happened... unless that's what you want. I don't want to do that either, but I will. For you."

Dante stared at Zane for a minute. His eyes burned as he held back tears.

"I think that would be for the best." Dante choked the words out, hating himself instantly. He turned as he said them, avoiding Zane's face. He left the room and was downstairs without knowing how he got there.

Across the room he spotted Linden, who looked nice and cozy with Ricky. They saw him and shot to their feet. Dante turned and headed for the front door. He weaved through people he'd never been introduced to. He skirted past Zane's friend, Vanessa and was outside, halfway down the driveway before Linden caught up with him.

He fell into step next to Dante and they were almost back to campus before Linden spoke.

"Did you want to get wasted?"

Dante stopped and looked at Linden. He blinked a few times, then wiped the tears off his cheeks. "Hell yes."

CHAPTER 11

ZANE

Zane dropped onto his bed and shut his eyes. Dante hadn't closed the door behind him, he'd bolted out of the room and away from Zane. He should've talked to him, or not. He shouldn't have done anything. He definitely shouldn't have kissed Dante.

But that kiss. Zane still felt breathless from it. His dick hadn't got the memo that they wouldn't be getting any and throbbed in his pants, still turned on by the way Dante had felt against him.

It had started off slow. Cautious. But perfect. Dante was soft and warm. Demanding, but not overwhelming. He'd seemed content to follow Zane's lead. But it had been the wrong thing to do. He'd known it before he did it, and kissed Dante anyway.

He kissed him, and freaked him out, and now Dante wanted him to pretend it never happened. And he would. He could. He'd feel the echoes of that kiss until the end of time, but he'd forget it, because Dante wanted him to.

Ricky appeared in the room and shut the door behind him. "Do you want to tell me what the hell happened?"

"I kissed him."

"I guessed that much."

"He wants me to forget it ever happened." Saying the words made it real. Zane had been dumped before. And it wasn't like him and Dante had been together, but somehow this hurt worse than any breakup he'd been through.

"It came out of left field for him. You've had weeks to get used to this."

Zane looked at Ricky. "I hate that you knew I liked him before I knew I liked him."

Ricky sat on the edge of Zane's bed, in the same spot Dante occupied a short time ago. The wrongness of it struck him, but he didn't say anything. He'd made a big enough fool out of himself that night.

"He'll come around."

Zane shook his head. "I'm not that guy, Ricky. I don't chase people. I don't badger them into doing things they don't want."

"What are you going to do?"

"What else can I do?" Zane shrugged. "I'm going to do what he asked and pretend it never happened. It's not a big deal."

"Are you sure about that? You could try talking to him tomorrow once he's had more of a chance to let this soak in."

Zane shook his head. "Nah. I think... I shouldn't have done it. It was stupid and impulsive." Zane flopped back on his mattress and stared at his ceiling.

"At least come back downstairs for a bit."

"Not really in the mood to party now, Ricky. But thanks."

"Don't sulk too long." Ricky left the room and shut the door behind him.

Zane grabbed his phone and stared at the screen. There were no texts from Dante. Not that he expected there to be any. He'd fucked up. Zane dragged a hand down his face and tossed his phone aside.

He stirred somewhere around three in the morning. Unaware that he'd fallen asleep, the stillness of the house was disorienting for a second. He woke feeling tragic, like a kicked puppy and it took a minute for the reason why to filter back into his brain.

"Fuck," Zane swore in the darkness. Blindly, he reached out and patted the bed until he found his phone. There were no texts from Dante. No missed calls. Nothing. Zane closed his eyes. "Shit."

Dante's silence bothered Zane more than a thousand angry texts would have. Over the past few weeks, being around Dante had felt good. Zane looked forward to seeing him. The fear that he might have caused irreversible damage to their friendship formed a knot in his stomach.

He wrote several different messages to Dante but erased each one instead of sending them. Eventually, he found the words he wanted to say and sent a message before he could second guess himself.

I won't let what I did change anything. I promise.

Zane rubbed his eyes and contemplated rolling over and trying to get more sleep when his phone rang. Shocked to see Dante's name on the screen, Zane swiped to answer.

"Dante?"

"I'm too drunk to text you," Dante whispered. Zane could hear the affect the alcohol had on Dante in the thick and heavy way he spoke.

"Are you okay? Are you safe? I can get you if you need a ride."

"I'm in my room. Linden got me drunk and tucked me in.

He just left. I have class tomorrow night. Make sure I don't miss class tomorrow, Zane."

"I promise."

"I'm too drunk to talk to you." Dante sighed.

"I meant what I said, Dante. I won't let what I did change anything, okay."

"That would be good. Yeah. No change. Can't lose if there's no change."

"Can't lose what, Dante?"

"I should sleep. Night Zane." The way Dante slurred and mumbled made Zane wonder if Dante would remember the phone call the next day. Because Zane was a man of his word.

He would forget about the kiss. He'd remember to stop by the dorm in time to get Dante up and ready for his class. He'd keep being his friend and he wouldn't let anything between them change.

When Dante opened the room to his dorm the next afternoon, Zane knew he'd have a hard time keeping all his promises. Dante's hair stood out in all directions. He was shirtless and his pajama pants hung low on his hips. Dante blinked at him.

"Zane?" Dante furrowed his brow. "What are you doing here?"

"I came with coffee and breakfast. Well, lunch."

"I don't.... what?" Dante blinked and rubbed his eyes.

Zane squeezed past Dante and shut the door. "Coffee and a bagel. I also bought a couple of those apple pies you like." He handed the coffee and the bag of food to Dante. "You don't remember that we talked last night, do you?"

Dante sat at his desk. He set the bag of food down but took a sip of the coffee. "Is it bad if I say no? I didn't embarrass myself, did I?"

"You asked me to make sure you made it to class today. That's all."

"Shit. What time is it?"

"It's a little after lunch. I figured you might need a few hours to shower the booze off and get your head on right."

Zane had to use all his strength not to stare at Dante's mouth. Now that he knew the taste of it, the way it felt under his. Now that the sound of Dante's breathing mingling with his had been seared into his brain, he'd have to work hard to not be a lovesick moron and stare at Dante.

"How'd you get into the state you were in last night?"

"Linden has a fake ID."

"Make sure that kid doesn't get you into any trouble." Zane frowned.

"Yes, Dad." Dante reached into the bag and grabbed an apple pie. He carefully opened the box and took it out. Zane watched Dante's eyes flutter shut as he took a bite.

"This is amazing. Oh my god," Dante said around a mouthful of food. "Holy crap. I need like ten more of these. I'm starving."

Despite his promise that nothing would change, things already had. He'd never felt awkward occupying the same space as Dante before. He'd been an idiot to think he could go around kissing people. He should've asked. Or kept his desire to himself. But even now, with his promise sitting between them like a brick wall, Zane wanted to smash it down and claim Dante as his own.

He wanted to make him smile and laugh. He wanted to be there for Dante, whatever he might need. But he'd promised. He had to pretend nothing changed. Despite Zane's urge to stick around and usher Dante into a shower, to make sure he ate all his food and got to class on time, the old Zane wouldn't have done any of that.

Zane motioned to the door. "I should go. I have to study, but I wanted to make sure you got to class."

"Thanks, Zane. I appreciate you coming by." Dante wouldn't meet his gaze.

"It's no problem. That's what friends do." Zane forced a smile and turned away. He reached for the doorknob. In his mind, Dante told him to wait. He stood and abandoned his pie on the desk. He'd ask Zane to turn around and then he'd kiss him. He'd weave his graceful fingers through Zane's hair and pull him into a kiss that tasted of coffee and apples.

Zane made it into the hallway without Dante calling out for him, and he left the dorm, and dreams of sugary kisses behind. To keep from being a liar, Zane went to the library. He had reading to catch up on and some research for an assignment. He walked down to the library and retrieved the materials he needed. After finding a quiet corner, Zane threw himself into his work.

Every time he stopped; he'd think of how stupid he'd been. Kissing Dante had been a mistake and promising to forget about it had been a fool's errand. Zane would never forget the way Dante melted into him or the way he made Zane feel light inside, like life was better with Dante close by.

Zane was engrossed in not thinking about Dante. He didn't notice someone approach until they dropped into the chair across from him. Zane looked up to see Ricky. He'd just come from class. He dropped his messenger bag on the floor and folded his arms over his chest.

"I haven't seen you stare at a book that hard since freshman year."

"I have a big assignment."

"Uh huh."

"I do."

Ricky frowned at him. "I know I'm a pain in the ass who changes partners the way most people change underwear, but you can talk to me, you know."

Zane sighed. "I know. I just... where do I start? There's a lot to unpack."

"Start at the beginning. Since when have you been into guys?"

Zane closed his book. "It's a new thing. I think sometime over the summer maybe. Then we got here and the more I've been around him, the more I've found myself noticing him. Kissing him was... an impulsive thing to do. Impulsive and stupid."

"He likes you. If someone looked at me the way he looks at you, I'd kiss them."

"It's complicated, Ricky. He's Jonathan's best friend, which makes him off limits. Not only that, my parents practically raised him. His mom works a lot, his dad is long gone, he has no other family. He has Jonathan, me and our parents."

"Shit."

"Yeah."

"What are you going to do?"

Zane shrugged. "The only thing I can do. Pretend it never happened."

"If you were interested, I could set you up with someone."

Zane shook his head. "No thanks. It's still all new to me, you know. I didn't ever think about guys or look at guys, and to be honest, I'm not sure if it's all guys, or just Dante. What's it like for you?"

"Me? I'm pan. I'm more attracted to people than what's in their pants. I've known that about me since I realized I had the hots for Cyclops and Storm. Superheroes were definitely the center of my sexual awakening."

"And Dante is the center of mine." Zane leaned forward and put his head on the table. "Fuck my life."

Ricky patted him on the back. "It's all a part of growing up."

"Please stop talking."

"Do you need the condom talk?"

Zane snorted and sat up. "Get the fuck away from me."

"You see, son, when a boy likes another boy…"

"I will give you ten dollars to not finish that sentence."

"You're so easy, Zane." Ricky nudged Zane's foot under the table. "Come on. I'll take you to the gym and we'll work out some of your frustrations."

"I'm not frustrated." Ricky simply stared until Zane deflated. "Fine. Okay. Fine. You win. Let's go to the gym. I'll pump the iron and get swole and then all my problems will be solved."

"You need a snack. You're hangry."

"I'm not hangry. I'm annoyed."

"You're cute when you're hangry." Ricky grabbed his bag off the floor and slid the strap over his shoulder. "Come on. Gym, then dinner. My treat."

"You're a pain in the ass," Zane said as he stood.

"I know."

Zane checked his phone as they made their way to the front of the library, but Dante hadn't sent him a single text. Zane tucked his phone away and hoped working out would make him too tired to keep obsessing. It was time to forget and move on.

CHAPTER 12

DANTE

Dante remembered the phone call. Everything about the night before was seared into his memory. He still couldn't believe Zane kissed him. Because he wanted to. Both facts blew his mind.

He thought Zane had been acting weird, but he never expected that kiss. That perfect moment where Zane stood close to him. Dante could still feel it if he closed his eyes. He'd thought about it all night. He'd cried on Linden's shoulder about it.

Dante didn't regret leaving the room. He was certain he made the right decision, but part of him wished he'd had stayed a little longer. For one more kiss. One more touch. One more moment where he got everything he wanted for a change.

The shower Dante had before class didn't do anything to wash away his disappointment. Regardless of Zane's promises, something had shifted between them. He'd felt it in the air when he'd appeared at Dante's door earlier. It made Dante happy that things didn't go back to normal so easily for Zane. His pride might never have recovered if Zane had been able to brush what happened aside quickly.

Never mind that Zane kissed him to begin with. Dante had no idea Zane was into guys. For a split second he thought he might be dreaming. But he wasn't. Zane had kissed him. And like a fool, Dante had begged him to forget all about it.

Now if only he could do the same thing.

Class was a waste of time for Dante, who struggled to pay attention and took almost zero notes. It was a stroke of luck that it was the class he shared with his roommate, Brant.

When class got out, Dante gathered his things and rushed to catch up to Brant before he disappeared.

"Hey, Brant, can I get a favor?"

Brant turned his head. "Sure, what's up?"

"Please tell me you took good notes today. I have two sentences and a doodle."

"I'll leave them on my desk if you want to copy them later." Brant shoved his things in his bag. "I have to run and meet the guys, right now, but we're going out later and I'll drop my shit off before then."

Brant didn't stick around long enough for Dante to thank him. Dante made his way to the cafeteria and grabbed an uninspiring dinner that sat heavy in his tender stomach. He'd done a number on himself the night before thanks to Linden's fake ID and way too much vodka.

Dante's phone sat silent in his pocket. Dante was used to Zane texting a couple times a day. Sometimes with a funny meme, other times to say hi or check in. But today the silence between them spoke volumes. He tried to ignore it and tell himself Zane needed time to wrap his head around what happened last night, then things could go back to normal. But Dante knew the truth. Things would never go back to the way they were.

His dorm was thankfully empty when he arrived. Dante dropped his bag on his bed and thought about curling up and going to sleep, it was how he usually dealt with unwanted emotions, but he had notes to copy and studying to do. Not that he knew why he was even in college to begin with. It seemed like the logical next step. That, and it got him out of his house.

Dante crossed the room to Brant's side. He'd said he'd leave the notes on the desk for him. Dante felt a bit weird about rifling through someone else's stuff, but he needed those notes.

"What are you doing?"

Dante turned to see Brant's girlfriend standing in the door.

"Brant said I could borrow some notes from class today. He said he'd leave them on his desk."

"You shouldn't touch shit that doesn't belong to you."

Dante glared at her. "What is your problem?"

"I don't think you should touch my boyfriend's stuff."

Before Dante could lose his shit, Brant came in.

"Did you know he was digging through your stuff?"

Brant rolled his eyes. "Relax, Kim." He walked over to the desk and moved his textbooks. "Here. Sorry."

"You said we'd have privacy," Kim whined.

Not interested in whatever was going to go down between them, Dante took the notes from Brant. "Thanks. I was heading out anyway."

Dante tucked the notes into his bag and exited the room. He paused in the hallway, able to barely make out some sort of disagreement going on between Brant and Kim. Dante wasn't in the mood to go to the library. He didn't want to be around people at all. He sort of wished he had a roommate who didn't seem to have an endless supply of time to fuck his girlfriend, because Dante would have liked to sink into a nice warm bed and forget about the past twenty four hours.

Dante pulled his phone out of his pocket and stared at it. His fingers curled around the hard plastic case and he trembled with the urge to throw it against the wall. That wouldn't help anything though.

Zane had lied.

He'd promised nothing would change, but his kiss had changed everything, and Dante didn't know what to do about all the feelings rolling around inside him. There were moments he felt calm, like a still pond in the morning, but most of the time he felt frozen in place as he watched the ocean recede, only for a wall of water to come rushing back at him.

Dante stared at the stairwell at the end of the hall. He tucked his phone away for now and went through the door. He took the stairs up to the roof and pushed the door open.

Instead of finding a nice, quiet place to think, an alarm screamed, deafening Dante and he pulled the door shut and raced back down the stairs two at a time. He made it almost to the main floor when his left ankle twisted. Pain shot up Dante's leg. He wasn't too hurt, but it felt like the wave finally made landfall and everything smashed into him all at once.

Dante sank down on the step and with a shaky hand, he pulled out his phone. He still wanted to throw it, or smash something, or scream, maybe even cry. Everything was fucked up now. Dante felt like he'd taken a kick to the chest. He couldn't get enough air.

He'd already lost everything. That's how it felt. How could he face Zane ever again, knowing what his lips felt like? And Zane had agreed too easily to forget about it. He probably regretted it. Dante stared at his phone and opened it to his contact screen. He stared at Zane's name, and he must have lost track of time because when the world came back into focus, he'd lost an hour.

Dante pushed himself to his feet and limped out onto the quad. Darkness had descended on campus and without his hoodie the autumn evening made him shiver.

Dante should've known the roof would be a bust, and now he had a headache, a heartache, wounded pride, and an ankle that throbbed like a heartbeat. He limped across the lawn, taking a small comfort in the fact that he hadn't run into anyone he knew.

"Dante?"

Dante rolled his eyes at the way he'd jinxed himself. He turned to see the girl Zane had introduced him to the other day.

"Um. Hey." Dante turned and tried to keep going, but with his limp he was no match for Vanessa, who was freakishly fast in her spiked shoes, despite the softness of the lawn.

"Are you okay?" She frowned at him and gave him the once over. Vanessa was pretty in a way that made you notice her, but also soft and friendly. She wasn't the sort of beautiful you couldn't approach. Her broad smile was friendly and the way she looked at you it made you want to talk to her.

"I'm fine." Dante tried to limp away.

Vanessa followed and slipped Dante's bag off his shoulder and onto hers. "Come on. The cafe isn't far. I'll get you some ice."

"I'll be okay." The look Vanessa gave him called his bluff and he sighed. "Actually, ice would be appreciated. Thank you."

His acquiescence brightened her mood. "How'd you get hurt?"

"It's stupid."

"Most injuries are. I once cut the tip of my thumb off with a mandolin." She held the digit up to show him. "Look, it's still flat there. I also have a scar down my leg from when I was in a six-skater pile-up. There might have been alcohol involved."

"Now I feel dumb and boring because all I did was step wrong. I was going down the stairs and my ankle rolled over like Rover."

Vanessa snorted. "I'm sorry. But yeah. Stairs are awful." Vanessa pulled the door to the cafe open and waited for Dante to hobble through. He found the nearest empty table and dropped into a chair.

Vanessa set his bag on the table. "I'll get some ice. Be right back."

"I'm not going anywhere." Dante

Vanessa returned a few minutes later with a towel filled with crushed ice. She set it on the table, then took the chair next to him. "Take your shoe off and let's see your ankle."

Dante popped his shoe off using the toe of his other foot, then lifted it so she could see. "It's probably nothing a day of rest won't fix."

Vanessa set Dante's foot on her lap and carefully pushed his pant leg up. She eased his sock down. "You're pretty swollen," she said with a frown. Carefully, she placed the ice on his leg. The cold had already started to seep through the towel and Dante flinched. "Sorry," Vanessa said.

"I want to forget this day ever happened."

"That good, huh?"

"Yeah. That good."

"Well, we've all had bad days, and we're all still here. That means we've survived every single thing life has thrown our way."

"That's one way to look at it."

Vanessa wasn't wrong, but her chipper attitude made it hard for Dante to sink further into his funk, which is where he wanted to be. If he couldn't go up to his room and sleep, he wanted to find a quiet place to sulk. He should've stayed in the stairwell.

"Hey, I think this belongs to you." Vanessa said to someone who had walked into the cafe.

There was only one person it could be and despite telling

himself not to look, he turned his head. Zane looked like shit. Which made Dante happy in a shitty and spiteful way.

"What happened?" Zane came to the table and instead of sitting down, he bent over and peered at Dante's ankle. Vanessa was kind enough to lift the towel to show him the damage.

Part of Dante wanted to act like a child and throw a tantrum, but the other part of him, the stupid mature part of him that reminded him he'd been given exactly what he asked for emerged.

"I rolled my ankle. It's no big deal."

"It's swollen," Zane argued, his brow furrowed.

"I'll be fine."

"He limped all the way here."

Thank you, Vanessa, for your support. "It's not the end of the world."

"You should take him to the clinic. They can have a look at it and maybe wrap it or something. I would have but I have to meet Noel." Vanessa carefully slid out of the chair. She handed Zane the ice-filled towel. "Sorry you've had a shitty day, Dante. I hope tomorrow is better."

Then she was gone, leaving Zane standing there staring down at him, water from the ice dripped from the towel onto the floor. "You're making a mess." Dante said, pointing to the towel.

"How shitty was your day?" Zane asked. He set the towel down on the table and frowned at Dante's ankle. "You should get that looked at."

"I'm fine." Dante pulled his sock up and his pant leg down. He slid back into his shoe and grabbed his bag. "I need some sleep. I'm tired, that's all."

If he'd thought he'd make a quick getaway, he'd been mistaken. A turtle could've gotten away faster than Dante.

"Let me take you to the clinic," Zane followed him out.

"I'm fine," Dante said through grit teeth. His ankle wasn't

the only thing that hurt, but his heart would need time to heal. Time, and distance from Zane.

"Dante, please." The tone in Zane's voice made Dante stop. He turned and looked at Zane. He studied him. The shadows under his eyes, the disheveled hair. The fucking sad sack, someone kicked my dog, look on his face.

"Please what?" Dante was afraid to ask, but afraid not to. This moment felt important. Maybe more important than the impulsive moment last night. They'd both had a day to think. To churn everything around in their heads and Dante didn't have to wonder if Zane felt as miserable as he did.

"Let me take care of you, okay?" Zane held his hand out. It hovered in the space between them and all Dante had to do was take it.

The same fears that sent him running last night came back. He'd lose everything. He'd be alone. He took a deep breath to steady himself. He'd had a preview of that life today. That empty, miserable existence absent Zane.

"Fuck it."

Dante took his hand.

CHAPTER 13

ZANE

Zane had spent the day gravitating between despair and anger. All self-directed, of course. He'd kissed Dante without thinking about it. The fall out made him feel like Icarus must have after he flew too close to the sun.

When Vanessa sent the text about Dante being hurt, of course his mind went to the worst-case scenario, and maybe that was the reason she sent the text she did. She'd been vague on purpose in her demand that Zane come to the cafe and get Dante, who was hurt.

And seeing him had been a punch to the guts. Dante looked as happy as Zane felt. And Zane knew then that things could never go back to normal between them. Not when Zane couldn't look at Dante without wanting him.

But Dante took his hand and Zane stepped closer to him. He wanted to pull him into his arms and hold him, that's all. He wanted to be close to him, to bury his nose in Dante's hair and memorize the way he smelled under his shampoo.

"Can you make it to my car?" Zane motioned to the space down the street he'd parked at.

Dante snorted. "It's not broken."

"I'm sorry. I feel like this is my fault."

"Well... you're not wrong." Dante's mouth fought a smile. "I tried to go up on the roof, but they armed the door. It freaked me out and I headed back down the stairs. Went a bit too fast for my own good and rolled my ankle going down the stairs."

Zane's stomach dropped. He gripped Dante's hand and urged him to follow him to the car. He didn't want to think about Dante falling down the stairs, but the image wouldn't leave his mind.

"I didn't know they armed the door."

Dante laughed. "Of course, you didn't." Dante squeezed Zane's hand. Watching Dante limp to the car made Zane want to pick him up and carry him, but he doubted Dante would appreciate it.

At the clinic, the nurse said it was nothing more than a bad sprain. Rest. Ice. Elevate. And stay off it as much as possible. She wrapped a tensor bandage around the injured ankle and sent them on their way.

Zane wasn't ready to let Dante out of his sight though. Not yet. Not before he had a chance to talk to Dante about what happened and what they were going to do. Where they were going to go from here.

"I don't want to take you back to your dorm." Zane admitted. "I think you should stay the night. Four flights of stairs are going to murder that ankle."

Dante leaned back with a sigh. "I didn't want to go back to my dorm either; and that was before I thought about the stairs."

"Stay the night? I think we should talk."

"What are we doing, Zane?"

"That's what we should talk about. Because whatever today was, I fucking hated it."

Dante exhaled. "Thank fucking god. Pretending that

nothing happened was a stupid idea and I'm sorry you listened to me."

Zane laughed. "Oh, is that how it's going to be?"

"Uh, yeah." Dante rolled his eyes. "Aren't you supposed to be older and wiser?"

"I'm not old enough to be wise, apparently. Let's stop and grab dinner on our way. Any preference?"

"Anything but pizza. Please no more pizza."

"I never thought I'd see the day when you got tired of it."

"It's everywhere. I get that it's good and easy but shit, branch out a little."

Zane stopped off at a local pasta place he frequented. He made Dante wait in the car while he bought dinner for them. He returned with a couple garden salads and chicken fettuccini for two. The side of garlic bread might come back to bite him later, because all he could think about was Dante on his bed, pinned underneath him, kissing Zane's breath away.

Zane handed the bag of food over to Dante and concentrated on getting home without popping another inappropriate boner. Zane had no idea what would happen between them, and though he didn't want to get his hopes up, he couldn't help it.

Kissing Dante had been the single most memorable moment of his entire life. Maybe Dante didn't want a repeat, and he had to be prepared for that. They rode the rest of the way in silence. Both content to exist in their own heads for a few minutes. Zane's hand itched with the desire to reach over and twine his fingers with Dante's.

That his place was empty when they arrived was a singular miracle. Dante hobbled inside and shut the door behind him.

"Did you want to eat down here or up in my room? I don't know when everyone else will be home."

"Upstairs is fine."

"Hang on one second." Zane took Dante's bag and slung it over his shoulder. With a firm grip on the takeout bag, he turned his back and crouched down. "Get on."

"I'm too old for piggyback rides."

"I'm not watching your busted ass hobble up the stairs."

"Fine. But I do this under protest." Dante wound his arms around Zane's neck and climbed up on his back. Zane stood and thanked his lucky stars he didn't have to take Dante far.

Zane carefully made his way up the stairs and took Dante all the way into his room before setting him down.

"I think I could get used to travelling like that." Dante sat on Zane's bed.

"If I give you piggy backs everywhere, maybe Ricky won't force me to go to the gym with him." Zane went to the head of the bed and arranged the pillows for Dante to lean against. "Here, sit back and relax. Put your foot up. I'll get some ice for you."

Dante scooted back and put his foot up as he was told. "The ice can wait. Can we eat? And maybe talk?"

Zane nodded and set the bag on the bed next to Dante. Zane climbed up on the bed and sat facing Dante.

They dug into the bag and Zane started with his salad, while Dante dug into the pasta.

"I knew you'd go for the noodles first."

"Hey, pasta is my life." Dante opened the container and stabbed his plastic fork into it, spearing the noodles. He brought the fork to his mouth and shoved it in. It wasn't careful or delicate, but Zane's dick didn't care. Dante doing anything with his mouth was suddenly a thousand percent erotic.

"So..." Dante said somewhere near the end of his pasta. They'd sat and ate in silence. The weight of his actions sat heavy on his shoulders. He knew what Dante tasted like, he knew he wanted more, and he was almost certain Dante did too. The way he looked at him sometimes gave Zane hope.

"I'm not sorry I kissed you." Zane put the lid on his half-eaten meal and set it on the nightstand. "I'm sorry I didn't listen to Ricky and go after you. I should have gone after you last night. Or this morning. Or anything. I should have done something."

"You did what I asked you to do." Dante whispered. "I... I wanted things to go back to normal because I didn't want to lose what I have. You and Jonathan, your parents, you've always been there for me."

"And we always will. This won't change that."

Dante looked Zane in the eyes. "It changed today. Today was like this black and white preview of what a future without any of you would be like, and it sucked." Dante bit his lip and Zane found a moment of bravery to reach for his hand.

Dante took it. They stared at the point of contact.

"I didn't mean to put you through this, but I don't know what happened, or when, but I can't stop thinking about you. And last night every time you were away from me it felt wrong. And I don't do the possessive caveman thing, but I wanted to last night with you."

Dante looked up at him and grinned. "That's kind of hot." His cheeks turned scarlet and he let out a breathless laugh.

"I don't know what came over me, but I can't get you out of my head."

"Do you want to?" Dante looked soft and vulnerable then. Zane tightened his grip on Dante's hand.

At one time the answer would have been yes. Zane would have found an excuse to not pursue this, whatever it was. "No."

"Then what do you want?"

"You're full of questions."

"You gave me a lot to ask about. I didn't even know you liked guys."

"I didn't. Maybe I still don't. You're the first one I've noticed. The first one I've wanted to kiss."

Dante exhaled. "One more question."

"Go ahead."

"Are you going to kiss me again?"

Elation bubbled up and made Zane want to straddle Dante. He wanted to grind their bodies together and lose himself in the feelings Dante brought out in him. "If you want."

"I want." Dante set his food to the side, then licked a bit of sauce off his thumb. "I have sauce breath." Dante shrank in on himself and it made Zane want to kiss him until he forgot to be shy about it.

Zane got off the bed and moved the food to the dresser.

"What are you doing?"

"Moving our dinner." Zane approached the bed and sat down next to Dante.

"I thought you were going to kiss me." Dante's lip stuck out in an adorable pout. Zane could get in a lot of trouble if Dante looked at him that way. He could easily see himself giving in to whatever Dante wanted.

"I am, but I plan on kissing you for a while, if that's okay."

"Yeah, but..."

Zane moved closer to Dante. He tangled their fingers together. It felt soft and natural, like it was something they'd always done.

"But?" Zane put his other hand on Dante's cheek.

"But I don't have a ton of experience."

Zane bit back a laugh. "And I do? Not that it matters. I liked kissing you for reasons that have nothing to do with how much or how little experience you have."

"I've kissed before. I don't suck." The way Dante flipped

between confident and shy gave Zane whiplash. He found it endearing, because around other people Dante would clam up and keep his thoughts to himself. But with every shaky admission, he let Zane in a little more.

"The only thing that matters to me is you. I don't want to say or do anything to make you run again."

Dante laughed. "After what I did to my ankle, I don't see myself running any time soon."

Zane narrowed his eyes at Dante. "Did you want me to kiss you or not? Because I'm trying hard to be perfect for you. Attentive and caring and all I want to do now is kiss you, so you'll stop—"

Dante leaned forward and pressed his mouth to Zane's. Dante's free hand slid up Zane's arm and across his shoulder. He didn't stop moving until his fingers curled around the back of Zane's neck.

Then Dante parted his lips and Zane's world tilted on its axis. Zane reached for Dante and he mirrored the way Dante held him. Dante led the kiss with his soft but eager movements. His tongue delved into Zane's mouth. Zane tasted him; the salty tang of the sauce was there, too.

Dante's fingers slid through the short hairs on the back of his neck, making him shiver. Dante's tender laugh melted Zane. "I'll have to remember that spot."

They stared at each other for a beat. "Are we doing this?" Dante asked.

Zane pulled him into another kiss. "Yeah. We are. I can pinch you if you think you're dreaming."

"Kissing is fine. Let's stick with that." Happiness glimmered in Dante's gaze and Zane swelled with pride because he was the cause.

"Your wish is my command." Zane kissed the smile off Dante's lips.

CHAPTER 14

DANTE

This was not how Dante pictured the day ending. He figured maybe he might sneak in a sad jerk off session before bed if his roommate went out, but Zane's mouth on his, his hand cupping Dante's face, was infinitely better.

Speaking of jerking off, Dante's dick throbbed in his pants, hard and needy. He didn't have a hair trigger. It would take a little more than the best make-out session on the planet to get him to come in his pants, but if Zane touched him, he knew he'd go off like a rocket.

Zane's kisses were better than Dante had imagined. And oh boy, had he imagined. Zane kissed like he meant it. His mouth moved in a way that was all confidence, but every time he pulled back and looked Dante in the eyes, he could see how uncertain he was. Zane had always worried about doing the right thing. Before, Dante had found it admirable, now it was downright adorable.

Zane stopped kissing him and he rested his forehead against Dante's. Dante listened to his ragged breathing and focused on the way Zane's hands seemed to want to explore Dante's body, but in little bursts of movement. Zane would caress his arm, then still. Then he'd move his hand up to Dante's neck and pause.

"So... what now." Dante desperately wanted to lock this down. He knew other people weren't fond of labels, but they eased his anxiety. He wanted a name for what they were doing. He hated guessing. "What are we?"

"We're whatever you want to be."

Dante laughed. "That's a non-answer. Whatever we are, we're both in this."

"I've never had a boyfriend before."

"I haven't had a girlfriend before. There's a lot of things I've never done before." Dante couldn't help but lick his lip. Zane's proximity had Dante feeling buzzed and giddy. He felt light-headed, like all the oxygen to his brain returned all at once.

"I think we should go slow." Zane's reply made Dante laugh.

"I didn't mean we should get naked and... you know... right now." Dante's face must have been as red as a tomato. "Slow is good, but like... are we telling people? Are we openly seeing each other? Are we keeping it a secret?" Dante took a breath. "Are we boyfriends?" He almost couldn't get the word past his lips. He felt like the fumbling virgin he was. Though Dante had had a boyfriend, that was a couple years before and they never got past the kissing stage.

"Jonathan is going to kill us," Zane said, though he didn't seem to be adversely affected by the realization.

"I think Jonathan will be fine with it."

"What makes you so sure?" Zane narrowed his eyes.

"Well, see, if we go out, and things work out, he'll have a brother he likes."

Zane laughed. "I hate that you're right." He leaned in and brushed his lips over Dante's. What Dante wanted was another make-out session, but Zane pulled back.

"How's your ankle?"

Dante frowned. "It's fine. You can play nurse later."

"Oooh. Nurse and patient. That's kinky." Zane waggled his eyebrows.

"There's something seriously wrong with you."

Zane reluctantly let go of Dante and stood. "I'll get some ice from downstairs."

Dante sighed and leaned against the stack of pillows Zane had arranged for him. After a minute, he rearranged himself and the pillows until he was laying down. The day had exhausted him and by the time Zane returned, Dante blinked his heavy eyelids.

"You look tired." Zane sat by Dante's feet and gently unwrapped his ankle before applying the ice pack.

"Today was the longest day in history."

"You should take my bed."

Dante was suddenly very awake. "Pardon?"

"Stay here. I'll take the couch if you want."

"What if I don't want you to sleep on the couch?"

"Then we sleep here."

"Okay." Dante's heart leapt into his throat.

Zane must have seen something like panic cross his face because he gave Dante's non-injured ankle a reassuring squeeze. "Just sleep. Maybe some cuddling and kissing. Don't worry, we're still taking things slow."

Dante's brain let out a sigh of relief, even if his dick wasn't on board with that idea. "Slow is good."

"Do you need something to sleep in?"

"Are you asking if I still wear pajamas?"

"There's nothing wrong with pajamas. Ricky walked around half of last year in a monkey onesie."

"I don't think I brought my onesie with me. I'll have to sleep in my underwear. Anyway," Dante said, desperate to change the subject. He'd never felt this awkward with Zane before. "How's the ankle looking?"

Zane lifted the ice pack. "A bit angry still. Swollen and it's starting to bruise now."

"Shit. I wrecked it."

"You'll be fine." Zane caught Dante's gaze. "You have a boyfriend to look after you now."

Dante's heart stuttered. "I do, do I?"

"Yeah." Zane put the ice pack aside and re-wrapped Dante's ankle in the tensor bandage. "Netflix?"

"Yeah."

Dante stood and took a deep breath. It was now or never. He peeled his shirt off and tossed it onto the floor. Then he undid his pants. He shoved them down past his ass and sat down on the bed to take them off the rest of the way. He kept his gaze down, not looking at Zane. Maybe Zane would change his mind about everything once he saw Dante half naked in his bed. Maybe he'd suddenly become un-bisexual. Maybe it had only been a short-lived phase of curiosity.

But when Dante got up the courage to get the rest of the way in bed, Zane stood there with a silly little grin on his face. He pulled his shirt off over his head and slid his pants down before kicking them aside. Then, he climbed into the other side of the bed and turned his television on.

Zane stretched an arm out to the side, a clear invitation for Dante if he ever saw one. Dante took a breath, then laid down. He curled into Zane's side and rested his head on Zane's chest.

It felt too good, too perfect, and entirely too easy. But sometime between choosing a show to watch and waiting for the other shoe to drop, Dante fell asleep.

He woke in the darkness and for a minute he didn't remember where he was. The room was cast in shadows and unfamiliar, then a breath of air puffed across the back of Dante's neck and he remembered that he was in Zane's room. In his bed.

Dante twisted around in Zane's arms and buried his nose into Zane's chest. He breathed him in, the scent of soap and familiarity encompassed him. Dante smiled and fell asleep again.

When he woke again it was morning and he knew exactly where he was and who he was with. Dante smiled at the sight of Zane's bare chest. Zane's leg moved and it brushed against Dante's cock. Dante sucked in a breath and tried to move away, but Zane's arm tightened.

"A little morning wood doesn't scare me." Zane sounded sexy when he first woke up.

Dante wondered if Zane was hard too. "How'd you sleep?" Dante asked. He didn't want to talk about morning wood, because then he might want to do something about it.

"Mmm. Fantastic." Zane's fingers dragged across Dante's shoulder. Dante allowed himself to burrow closer to Zane. "How about you? How'd you sleep? How's the ankle?"

"I slept good." He'd liked sleeping next to Zane more than he thought he would. As far as sleepovers went, he'd absolutely want a repeat. "The ankle is... not bad, I think. I'll see how it goes when I try to walk."

"When's your first class?"

Dante frowned. "Ten. What time is it?"

"A little after eight. You should shower while I get us some breakfast."

"I have nothing to wear. Can I at least borrow a clean shirt? Or a hoodie?"

Zane laughed and kissed the top of Dante's head. "Not even one day in and you're already angling to steal my clothing."

"You have the best clothes."

"I don't know, the shirt you wore to the party looked amazing on you."

"Yeah?"

"Hell yeah. But you're cute in everything. It's not fair."

"Compliments will get you everywhere."

"A shower will get you bacon and eggs."

"With cheese?"

"With cheese." Dante forced himself to sit up. He pried himself away from Zane and swung his legs over the edge of the bed. He stood slowly, unsure how his ankle would feel after a night of not moving.

"How's it doing?" Zane asked as he pulled a shirt on.

"It's... tolerable. I don't want to tap dance or anything, but I think I'll be okay."

"Good." Zane dug in his dresser and pulled out a shirt and a hoodie. He passed them to Dante and brushed a kiss against his lips. "I'll brush my teeth and get you an extra towel, then you can shower." Zane started to move away from Dante but smiled and turned back to steal another kiss.

Zane's shower was miles better than the ones in the dorms. For one, he had privacy. For another, the water heated to a decent temperature, and the best part of all was that Zane was downstairs with fresh coffee and breakfast when Dante got done.

Because of the quiet night they'd had together, Dante had half expected a quiet morning together, but when he got downstairs, most of Zane's roommates were home. Ricky was at the stove, helping Zane cook, Noel was at the table nursing a cup of coffee while Ricky complained about a speeding ticket, he'd got the night before.

"If you'd stop speeding, you'd stop getting tickets." Zane supplied. His gaze slid over and met Dante's and Dante caught the hint of a smile playing at his lips.

"Bite me, Obi-wan." Ricky said.

"I'd rather bite you." Zane reached for Dante and pulled him close. He brought his mouth down onto Dante's and kissed him in front of all his friends. Dante was too stunned to respond. It felt important that Zane would jump in with both feet. Like it wasn't an experiment at all, and Zane was sure about them. "You smell good." He leaned in and traced the shell of Dante's ear with his nose. "You smell like me."

"I used your shampoo," Dante admitted.

"Sit down, I'll get you a plate."

Dante hobbled over to the table and dropped into a chair.

None of Zane's roommates commented on Dante's presence, or their intimate embrace, but he did see a few subtle smiles and Ricky waggled his eyebrows at Dante, which made him blush.

Zane set a plate down for Dante as his phone chimed with a text. His heart caught in his throat when he saw that it was Jonathan who sent him a text message.

Zane glanced at Dante's phone screen. "Are we telling him?

Dante opened his mouth, then shook his head. "Not yet." Dante didn't want to hide things from Jonathan, but he needed time to wrap his own head around what was happening with him and Zane first.

Zane nodded and Dante didn't know if he looked relieved or not by Dante's decision.

CHAPTER 15

ZANE

Zane took Dante to his first class and kissed him goodbye in the hallway. The newness of his relationship had him walking on cloud nine. He'd fought the urge to pin Dante against the wall and kiss him properly, the way he burned to kiss him.

Dante looked sexy as hell wearing Zane's hoodie. It was too big on him but seeing Dante wear it made Zane happy. He knew he didn't own Dante, but it made it look like Dante belonged to him, and he found he liked that.

Zane had classes later which straddled Dante's and they wouldn't be able to see each other for the rest of the day, but maybe Zane could convince Dante to have a late dinner with him again. Maybe he could convince Dante to stay the night.

Zane was fucked. Incredibly fucked. But he couldn't bring himself to mind. Sleeping next to Dante had been amazing and he found himself wanting to tangle himself up in Dante all day long. He wanted to keep him close, to rub himself all over Dante like a cat.

Zane returned home to study until his next class, but Ricky followed him up the stairs and made himself at home on Zane's bed. It was something he'd always done. He'd flop down on the mattress. Sometimes he'd curl up under the covers and talk at Zane while he tried to work. Today, seeing Ricky in his bed felt wrong. That had been where he'd spent the night with Dante curled up in his arms.

"Glad to see you went after him."

"I don't think I had a choice."

Ricky shrugged. "There's always a choice."

Zane rolled his eyes. "Why are you in here? I have to study."

"I wanted to say congratulations. Happy looks good on you. I must say, you're adjusting well to the whole not-straight thing."

Zane shrugged. "Does it have to be a big deal?"

"You don't have any angst at all about joining the dick-side."

Zane groaned. "You didn't just call it that."

"Oh, but I did. I'm very punny."

"Get out of my room. I don't know you."

Ricky rolled off Zane's bed and ruffled his hair. Zane pulled away and smoothed his hair back down.

"My little boy is growing up."

"There's nothing little about me and you know it." Zane gave Ricky a playful shove. "I have work to do. Get out of here."

"Okay, fine. But speaking of big, make sure you properly prepare that cute little boyfriend of yours. You don't want to split him in half. It's not as fun as it sounds."

"Stop talking about my boyfriend."

"Man, I take it back. Happiness looks good on you, but you're fucking cranky and possessive." A broad grin flashed across Ricky's face. "I hear sex is a good mood booster."

"Get—" Zane started to say but Ricky already disappeared into the hallway and pulled Zane's door shut behind him.

Ricky's offhand remarks stayed with Zane all day. By the time Zane finished his last class and was free to meet up with his boyfriend, he'd worked himself into a state of anxious desire.

Sex was something Zane had always enjoyed. When he was younger, he mostly cared about his own orgasms, but as he grew older and gained more experience, he discovered the pleasure he could find in pleasing his partner. But when it came to having sex with a guy, Zane was out of his element.

Dante limped out of his building and Zane frowned at the exhaustion etched onto his face.

Zane closed the distance between them. His breath hitched at the way Dante's face lit up when he saw Zane. He flung his arms around Zane and buried his face into Zane's chest.

"Miss me?" Zane asked, brushing a kiss against the side of Dante's head.

Dante nodded.

"You're limping." Zane held Dante tighter.

"Walking is stupid. I want a hoverboard."

"I don't have a hoverboard, but I can piggyback you to my car and we can get something to eat."

Dante looked up at him. "Okay, but you have to kiss me first."

Zane had no trouble fulfilling that wish. Already he was addicted to Dante, even if he was too fucking scared to do more than kiss him. He didn't even have the courage yet to do half the things he wanted. Not yet. Zane had been serious about taking things slow.

After a whole day spent being around people, they were content to sit at the empty end of a parking lot and eat burgers from a drive-thru in Zane's car.

"I think you should let me crash at your place again," Dante said.

Zane was surprised at the boldness of his boyfriend. But he

liked this side of Dante. The self-assured way Dante carried himself acted like an aphrodisiac.

"Yeah? You do?"

"Well, I could use the elevator in Cavell, but that thing shudders like it's going to fall down the shaft and kill me. I don't trust it."

"So dramatic."

"Did it work?"

Zane leaned across the seat. He slid his hand through the hair at the back of Dante's neck and pulled him in for a kiss. He meant it to be a chaste kiss, a taste, but Dante was too easy to get tangled up in. Dante turned in his seat and wound his arms around Zane's neck.

He wanted to take Dante back to his place and do this where he could stretch out over Dante and pin him in place. Where he could enjoy the feel of their bodies sharing heat.

Zane pulled away and smiled back at Dante, whose cheeks were rosy. He looked at Zane with stars in his eyes and his fingers brushed through the hairs on the back of Zane's neck. Zane shivered.

"Yeah, you can stay at my place. Whenever you want." It wasn't realistic, but he imagined Dante moving in. He pictured them waking up together every morning, a mass of limbs and lust.

Dante leaned in and stole a kiss. "I knew you'd see it my way."

Zane had a feeling he'd be seeing a lot of things Dante's way. "Do you need anything from your dorm?"

"I have the essentials in my bag."

Zane laughed at the sheepish expression on Dante's face. "You planned this."

Dante shrugged a shoulder and Zane watched a brick of his walls slip back into place. He gripped Dante's face in his hands and pulled him close. He slanted their mouths together. Kissing Dante was the easiest, most natural thing in the world. He loved the way Dante surrendered to him, the way he'd touch Zane, his fingers pulling on Zane's shirt, or his hair, or gripping into his flesh.

"I like that you planned it." Zane whispered when he pulled away.

"Let's get out of here."

Nothing had ever sounded so good to Zane.

They prepared for bed side by side in the upstairs bathroom. Noel was at work and Ricky had been holed up in his room most of the day working on assignments. The only sign that anyone else was in the house was the low and steady thud of Ricky's music.

Dante climbed into Zane's bed and burrowed down under the covers. His hair was already mussed, and he looked entirely too sweet. Zane's heart pounded in his ears, a powerful a rush of blood and desire that made his head swim.

He turned out the lights and crawled under the covers. Unlike the night before, they didn't pretend they were going to watch television or sleep. Zane stretched out next to Dante and propped himself up on one elbow. Dante burrowed closer, practically wedging himself underneath Zane.

Zane closed his eyes when Dante ran his hands up Zane's sides and over his chest. His delicate touch caressed the sides of Zane's neck and urged him to lower himself down into a slow, tantalizing kiss.

Their lips parted. The earth stopped moving. Time and life ceased to exist. Dante's plump lips and supple mouth were the only things left that mattered. Dante's fingers twitched in Zane's hair as Zane rolled over, sliding on top of Dante. He covered Dante with his body and pressed him into the mattress.

Being close to someone had never felt this big. Zane was

about to come in his briefs just from kissing Dante. He took a breath and buried his face in the crook of Dante's neck. His tongue poked out of his mouth, unbidden, and tasted the flesh below Dante's ear.

Dante sucked in a breath. His hands slid down Zane's sides until he came to his hips. Dante gripped him and arched up, pressing their erections together. Zane nearly shot right there.

He pressed his open mouth against Dante's throat and gave his hips an experimental thrust. There was something gloriously obscene about the way it felt when their cocks touched. Even through the fabric of their briefs, the evidence of Dante's arousal made Zane quiver with want.

He devoured Dante's mouth. His tongue sought, and was granted, entry. Underneath him, Dante panted and moaned. Zane ate every gasp, every sigh and whimper like he'd been starving his whole life.

Dante's hands blazed a trail of heat down Zane's back. He gripped Zane's ass in his hands and held them together. Zane thrust harder and faster, the friction heated Zane until he thought he'd burn up.

When Dante came, Zane thought he'd die. It was the hottest thing he'd ever felt. Dante arched up into him and ground against him. Their cocks rubbed together, and Dante's ragged breaths turned into a sound Zane had never heard him make before. It was thin, light, and high pitched. The whimper broke into fragments that punctuated the silence of the room.

Zane was certain he could feel the dampness of Dante's release. Heat flashed through him, hot and sudden. His toes curled, and he moaned into Dante's mouth, surrendering to the tidal wave of release crashing crashed into him.

Eventually, Zane had to stop thrusting, stop moving. Stop anything that wasn't breathing and clinging to Dante. He let himself collapse on top of Dante, who didn't seem to mind.

Dante wrapped his arms around Zane and kissed the top of his shoulder as he tried to catch his breath.

"I'm not sure I like coming in my underwear, but I'm also not sure I don't like coming in my underwear. I'm very torn. But as much as I love having you on top of me, I need to breathe."

Zane rolled onto his side. "That was..."

"Mind blowing. Amazing. Stupendous. Earth shattering. Take your pick."

Zane kissed Dante through a laugh. "You're chatty after you come."

"I have no energy left to filter myself. I don't have the energy to get out of these gross underwear either."

Zane threw the covers off. "Your wish is my command."

Dante's face flushed crimson and he bit his lower lip. As much as Zane loved chatty, post orgasm Dante, he hoped Dante wouldn't ever stop blushing for him.

CHAPTER 16

DANTE

"I thought you died."

Dante turned his head at the sound of Brant's voice. He'd been tucked away in the library since Zane dropped him off there before he went to class. He'd used his time wisely and was putting the finishing touches on an assignment before he turned it in.

"Uh. That's dramatic, but okay. Oh." Dante turned and dug in his bag and pulled out the notes he'd borrowed from Brant. "I can't believe people still take notes with a pen."

"I absorb things better this way." Brant took the notes back, folded them, then shoved them into his back pocket. "I'm sorry about Kim. She was rude."

Dante blinked and searched his mind for what Brant was talking about. "Oh, about the notes? It's fine. I'd forgotten." He'd been wrapped up in Zane until he didn't have room in his head for much else.

Dante thought of what they'd done together. It was the most Dante had ever done with another person. He'd orgasmed before, but by his own hand, alone. Being with Zane like that felt huge, and the way he took care of him after. He'd cleaned the cum off Dante, which got him hard all over again, but he was tired, and he wanted to enjoy the quiet aftermath of the most beautiful experience of his life.

Zane didn't push for more, either. He'd climbed back into bed and wound his arms around Dante. They talked for a while, until their voices grew thick with sleep and exhaustion swept them into the darkness.

Brant's laughter snapped Dante out of his dreamy haze.

"Someone got laid."

Dante opened his mouth, then closed it again.

"Relax, it's not like I want details, but I know that dopey look anywhere."

"It's pretty new."

Brant stood. "I have to get to practice. I wanted you to know that Kim won't be rude to you anymore. She's not a bad person, she doesn't people well, and it comes out all wrong sometimes."

Dante nodded. Truth be told, he'd barely noticed Kim or her behavior toward him. Dante was too used to keeping his head down and his mouth to himself. He was used to being weird around people. "Tell her I get it."

Brant looked relieved. "Thanks, Dante." Brant's phone beeped and he reddened. "I'm officially late."

"Better run."

Brant left Dante with a lot to think about. He knew what it was like to be awkward around people. He'd had more success lately breaking out of his shell, but for the most part, Dante still played a wall-hugging lurker. Someone content to be overlooked instead of being in the spotlight.

And Zane had still noticed him. Dante would never understand why, but he wasn't about to try and dig for the reasons why. His lips curved into a smile and he got back to his assignment.

His phone buzzed as Dante limped across the quad. He

pulled his phone out and answered Jonathan's call. His smiling face filled the screen. "What's up, buddy? I need validation. Tell me you miss me."

Dante grinned. "Not even a little."

"I hate you."

"You don't."

"Okay, I don't."

They talked about Los Angeles and the pictures of the art projects currently consuming Jonathan's existence. Dante carefully kept the conversation about Jonathan. It made him feel like a liar and a shitty friend. Jonathan had always been there for Dante and he had no reason to believe that Jonathan would mind Dante dating his brother, but for now, Dante didn't want to risk it. And as selfish as it was, he wanted to keep Zane to himself for a while longer. Soon enough the cat would have to come out of the bag, but Dante would cross that bridge when they came to it.

"See more of that campus hottie you were telling me about?"

Dante hated facetime. It gave too much away. He watched his cheeks turn crimson. "You could say that."

"Sounds serious." Jonathan's face softened into something that looked like happiness. Jonathan had always been protective of him. He urged him to be more outgoing and tried to get him to make friends. He'd tried to set him up on dates a couple times, but Dante refused to let his best friend play matchmaker. He wondered if Jonathan would still be happy if he knew who Dante was seeing.

"It's too new to be anything but new." Dante bit his lip. "I don't want to jinx it."

Jonathan rolled his eyes. "Okay, be a hold out. It's not like I wanted juicy details."

"Good, because I'll never tell."

Jonathan's eyes widened. "Never? I told you about Catherine and the great bleacher blow job."

"And that's a story I never needed to hear. Has anyone told you that you over share?"

Jonathan pretended to think. "Um. No."

"Well, it's true."

Dante's ankle throbbed as he made his way to the cafe where he hoped to convince Zane to meet him. He knew they couldn't spend every waking moment together, but the need to see him flooded Dante's veins.

"If it isn't my favorite freshman." Zane appeared out of nowhere and threw his arm around Dante's shoulders.

"Hey, Zane. You're just in time to say hi to Jonathan."

Zane didn't miss a beat. He didn't move his arm, however, and Dante sort of liked that he kept it in place. Like touching Dante wasn't taboo. "Hey little brother."

"Have you met the mysterious guy Dante is crushing on?"

"Holy shit, Jonathan." Dante nearly choked on his tongue.

"I haven't."

"We need to find out if he's a creep."

"Hello. I'm right here. I can vouch for his non-creepiness."

"Don't worry about a thing, Jonathan. I'll kick the guy's ass myself if he fucks with Dante."

"You better. He's basically your little brother, too you know."

If Dante got any more uncomfortable, he would need to find a hole to crawl into. Zane's grip on his shoulder tightened, as if he shared Dante's discomfort.

"I'm taking good care of Dante. In fact, I was about to drag his ass over to the dining hall to eat with me."

"You guys do know I'm right here. And I'm an adult. I don't need babysitters."

"If we don't watch out for you, no one will."

The truth of Jonathan's words put a spear through Dante's heart. His mom didn't care about him. He hadn't thought much about her lately, but beyond her sporadic texts, he hadn't heard from her since he left home.

"Hey... you okay?" Jonathan asked.

"Yeah, just hungry."

"See, you do need a keeper," Jonathan crowed.

"Hungry. Hanging up now," Dante said. He promised Jonathan he'd call him later and ended the call. When his phone sat safely in his pocket, Zane pulled Dante to a stop. He turned to face him and tugged him into a kiss.

"Hi," Zane said when he pulled away. He slid his hand into Dante's and pulled him in the direction opposite of the dining hall.

"Hi." Dante frowned. "I am hungry." He tried to tug Zane back in the direction of food, but Zane wouldn't be moved.

"I figured. That's why we're going out to dinner."

"I thought we were going to the dining hall?"

Zane laughed. "My baby deserves better than cafeteria food on a date."

Dante's insides turned to fireworks. "Date?"

"Yeah." Zane looked at him. He gave him one of his wide, handsome smiles, the kind that made his eyes light up. Dante's stomach did a swoop at the knowledge that he was the person who put it there.

"Is this your first date?" Zane asked when they were in the car, enroute to their destination.

"No. I've dated a little."

Zane sighed. "Thank fuck," his peel of laughter surprised Dante. "It was a last-minute decision and if it was your first, I'd have to cancel and do it right." He glanced at Dante with narrowed eyes. "Who was your first date? I feel like I should have paid attention to this."

"Tommy Miller."

"You went out with Tommy?"

"We went out once. We met at the theater and he didn't ask me out again when I refused to let him blow me in the back row." Dante cringed at the memory.

"Well, I'm sorry your first date sucked. If it helps, my first date was Misty Paulson and her mother escorted us. Sat at a nearby table at the restaurant. Sat a few rows behind us at the theater. It was stressful."

"Poor Misty."

"Poor Misty? Poor Zane! I couldn't even look at Misty without her mom giving me the death stare."

"Well, look at it this way. If her mom hadn't chaperoned, you might have married Misty. You'd have three point seven kids and a pack of poodles by now."

"That's a no from me. Marriage I wouldn't rule out, and kids... the jury is still out on them, but the poodles are a hard limit."

"What, you want a manly dog? Something big enough to eat someone's face."

"I want cats. At least they have the decency to wait until you're dead to eat your face."

A laugh bubbled out of Dante and despite his effort to stop it, he snorted. "This is the best date I've ever been on and we haven't even got to where we're going yet."

Zane reached over and gave Dante's hand a squeeze. "If you die before me, I promise to keep the cats from eating your face."

Dante couldn't wipe the smile off his face. Zane had only been joking, but his words implied they'd be together forever, or at least long enough for corpses and cats to be a concern for them.

He'd never imagined the mention of corpses on a date would be romantic, and maybe it shouldn't be. Maybe it was too morbid and weird, but it pleased Dante in a way he couldn't describe that Zane thought they'd still know each other when they were old enough to worry about such things. Death was such an abstract concept. Something Dante knew about but had yet to experience in any tangible way.

"You got quiet." Zane pulled into a parking space on the street and killed the engine.

"I was thinking about our corpses."

Zane's eyebrows arched into his hairline, then he flashed Dante a smile. "You're cute when you're morbid."

"I can't stop thinking about cats eating our faces."

"How macabre."

Dante shrugged. The certainty that he fucked up their date was enough to choke him. It was why he stayed quiet and didn't talk to people. But Zane wasn't people. He was Zane.

"I think it's sweet that you want to be around me until I'm a corpse."

Zane's smile softened and he leaned across the front seat, drawing Dante into a kiss that felt sweeter than any kiss Zane had given him before. "I plan on being around you for a long time."

Something warm bloomed in Dante's core and he knew then that this had to work. He couldn't lose Zane. Not now. Not ever. He was so in love with him that it made his head spin. Dante reached for him and pulled him into a kiss so sudden and deep it curled his toes. His fingers curved and cupped the sides of Zane's face.

"Dante," Zane panted.

"Can I get a raincheck on the date?" Dante looked at Zane and hoped he understood what he wanted, what he needed from him. Because if he had to spell it out, he would, but he didn't know how to say it without sounding like a stupid, love-sick, virgin.

Take me home. Make me yours. Love me. Keep me.

Zane kissed him again, slow, soft and full of promise. "Raincheck," he whispered against Dante's mouth before pulling away and starting the car.

Dante put his hand on Zane's thigh and left it there as Zane drove home.

CHAPTER 17

ZANE

Dante's lust for Zane was heady. He'd never had someone, anyone, look at him the way Dante did, with wide eyed fascination one moment and hooded want the next. The rush of power filled Zane as he took Dante home.

Uncertainty thrummed under Zane's skin, though. Thick and unwelcome, he tried to choke it down, tried to push it aside, or swallow it. He wanted to give Dante what he wanted. Everything he wanted. He didn't want to make Dante wait, but there were some things Zane wasn't ready for. And he wasn't ready for what Dante wanted.

Dante wanted to have sex and Zane did too. God, he practically came in his pants just thinking about Dante's pupils blown wide, his parted, panting lips, and his trembling body as Zane would sink inside him.

But Zane wasn't ready. He wanted it more than anything. But before they did anything else, before they crossed that line, Zane had to visit a clinic. He had to protect Dante. He had to figure out how to do it, how to love him without hurting him. Because Zane would rather walk on broken glass than hurt Dante.

He didn't have the guts to burst Dante's bubble until they were up in Zane's room and Dante's hands slid tentatively under Zane's shirt.

"I know what you want, Dante, and we will. But..."

The pain of rejection flickered in Dante's eyes and Zane cupped his cheeks and kissed him. He backed him up against his bedroom door and wedged a knee between Dante's trembling legs.

"I want you so much, but not tonight. Not yet." Not until Zane knew he could make it good for Dante. He didn't like feeling this way, this insecure and uncertain.

"Why?" Dante asked, though Zane guessed from the way he winced, he hadn't wanted to.

Zan peppered the corners of Dante's mouth and down his jaw with tender kisses. "Because I want to wait. I need to get tested, Dante." Zane exhaled. "I've always used condoms, but I want to be sure we're safe. That you're safe."

Dante sighed. "I hate it when your logic means depriving me of having my own way."

Zane laughed and leaned in, caging Dante against the door. A rush of something... power maybe... danced up his spine. Dante was shorter than him. Smaller. And he was pinned against the door at Zane's mercy. He could get away whenever he wanted, but Dante writhed against Zane's thigh, proving how much he didn't want to get away.

Dante's willing confinement turned Zane on, and he reached down, grazing the bulge in Dante's pants with his hand. "But that doesn't mean I'll let you suffer, babe."

Dante wrinkled his nose, despite the whoosh of air that left his lungs. "Your terms of endearment need work."

"Why are you sassy with me and quiet with everyone else?" Zane leaned in and tasted the patch of skin below Dante's ear.

He scraped his teeth across the tender flesh and bit back a smile when Dante twitched in his arms.

"You," Dante panted, and Zane took pride in the way he could scramble Dante's circuits. "You make me safe."

Zane's eyes fluttered shut and if he could, if he knew how, he'd bury himself inside Dante at this very moment. He'd sink between his cheeks, into a place no one else had ever touched him, and he'd claim him. It made him feel like a caveman, not in a—let me knock you over the head and take you to my cave—sort of way. More like a possessive, mono-syllabic, destroy-anything-that-threatens-what's-his, way.

Zane's fingers trembled. What if he wasn't good at this? What if he didn't get it right? Then he smiled as Dante kissed him and moaned into his mouth. He pushed his hand into Dante's pants, sliding it under the band of Dante's briefs until he took hold of Dante's cock.

Dante squeaked. His fingers dug into Zane's hips.

Zane liked Dante's cock. It was average, like Dante, but it felt good in Zane's hand. Hard and hot. Velvety and smooth, and wet. Beads of precum leaked from the tip. Zane hadn't touched another guy before Dante, and he didn't want to touch another one after him.

"Zane. Zane... I'm gonna..."

"Do it," Zane growled, increasing his speed. He crushed his mouth to Dante's and jacked him faster and harder. Dante writhed against him, chasing the friction, fucking himself with Zane's hand. And then Dante was coming. Zane pulled back, breaking their kiss to watch him.

Dante's eyes squeezed shut and his whole face turned pink. His ragged breathing hitched, and he swore as he came, coating Zane's hand in hot, sticky cum. His fingers gripped Zane's hips hard enough to bruise, but he didn't care. He'd wear any mark Dante put on him with pride.

"I think my bones melted." Dante leaned into Zane.

Apparently, the bones in Dante's arms and hands hadn't melted. Zane's entire being zeroed in on the tentative touch that snaked across his hip, following along the bare skin at the top of his pants. Dante's touch asked the permission that wouldn't seem to come out of his mouth.

"Go ahead," Zane breathed into Dante's ear. "Only if you want."

"I want." Dante's laugh was light and thready, breathless. Zane had done that. He kissed Dante's head and breathed in the soap scent still clung to him.

Dante fumbled with the button on Zane's pants. The rasp of the zipper sounded like a bomb going off in the quiet room, then Dante's unsure fingers moved over Zane's cock.

"I've never..." Dante started to say, and Zane laughed.

"I haven't either. Go with your gut."

"What if it doesn't feel good?"

Zane huffed out a quiet laugh. "It already feels good, Dante."

Dante's hand gently closed over Zane's cock. The fabric felt like a brick wall, keeping Zane from his goal, his prize, his treasure. Then Dante's hand moved, and the fabric heated. The friction burned in an unexpected and delicious way.

"Fuck, Dante. Touch me." Zane wasn't above begging.

Dante tried to twist his wrist to slide his hand in Zane's pants the way Zane had done to him, but his shorter stature made the angle awkward. Zane let go of Dante long enough to shove his pants and underwear down, granting his boyfriend all the access he needed.

Zane couldn't look away. He was mesmerized by the sight of Dante's hand on his cock. He held him lightly, almost too light, but after a few test strokes, his grip increased with his confidence. Zane was sure his knees were melting.

"Feels good. Holy shit." Zane braced his hands on the door to keep himself from grabbing Dante, flinging him down on the bed and rutting against him like an animal.

Zane's gaze flicked to Dante's face. He had his bottom lip clamped in his teeth. He stared at Zane's dick as though it were his last meal. "Dante, fuck."

Dante's grip twisted and he swirled his thumb over the head of Zane's cock. The orgasm that hit him then rocked him to his core. There was no warning. He'd been enjoying the rise of pleasure, the heat of the moment, the intensity of Dante's expression and the intimacy they shared. Then with one simple touch, Dante had sent Zane shooting over the edge.

Zane, still coming, still trembling, still needing oxygen, shoved his tongue into Dante's mouth and kissed him until he felt like his bones had also melted.

"Dante." Zane pulled away and sighed. "That was. Wow. Shit. Fuck yes."

Crimson slashed across Dante's cheeks and he held up his cum slick fingers. "Do you have um... what do I do with this?"

Zane, without thinking, flicked his tongue out and licked a blob of rapidly-cooling cum off Dante's fingers. Dante's eyes widened and Zane had to use all his energy to not wince at what he'd just done.

"That was..."

"I don't know why I did that," Zane admitted.

"It was hot." Dante looked as embarrassed at the admission as Zane had felt at the act.

Zane pecked Dante on the lips. "Go clean up, then get your books out and I'll whip something up for us to eat."

"Bossy." Dante eyed Zane with obvious interest as he tucked his dick back in his pants.

"What kind of a boyfriend would I be if I didn't make sure you had time to do your work?"

Dante rolled his eyes, but the smile on his face told a different story. "Fine. Fine. Have it your way."

Zane followed Dante to the bathroom, where they shared the sink to wash their hands. He stole a kiss then went downstairs to raid the fridge. It was probably for the best that he hadn't taken Dante out to dinner that night. His bank account wasn't in the best shape. He whipped up a couple turkey, cheese, and mayo sandwiches, putting extra mustard on Dante's, even though Zane himself couldn't stand it. He wondered if he'd mind kissing Dante if his mouth tasted like the offensive yellow condiment.

Zane smiled and took the food upstairs to his boyfriend, determined to see for himself.

Zane entered the library after walking Dante to class. Midterms were next week, and he had a lot of studying to do to catch up. He'd been wrapped up in Dante for the past few weeks, and as amazing as it had been, he'd let a few things slide.

He found a quiet corner of the library to sit down in and opened his laptop. He queued up his playlist and shoved his earbuds in, then signed into the student portal to check his grades.

Zane's heart sank. He'd missed a paper. He remembered the day it had been assigned. The day Dante had hurt his ankle. The day after Zane kissed him. Zane's professor wasn't the forgiving type. He was a stickler for punctuality and rules. There was no way he was going to let Zane hand it in late, especially considering he'd need more than a one or two-day extension. He was fucked. Unequivocally.

He buried his face in his hands. He tugged at his hair, then shot an email off to his professor, begging for extra credit, or an extension. Even if Zane had to stay awake for thirty-six hours and mainline caffeine, he'd do it to get his work in.

While he waited for a response, Zane got to work on the missed assignment, if he got the extension, he'd need every moment he could get. Which meant that he'd have to cancel his plans with Dante.

Zane felt disgusted with himself and his inability to focus and balance his life appropriately. It's why he hadn't been serious about anyone. He hadn't wanted to. But Dante was different. Everything about the way he felt for him was unlike anything he'd felt before.

But if Zane got too busy thinking with his dick to get through the last year of college, he'd be useless to Dante. To anyone. Zane needed his degree, needed a job. He must focus.

Zane checked the time. He had two hours until Dante got out of class. It wasn't a lot of time. Somehow, he had to find the words to explain to Dante he didn't want to break up, but they'd been spending too much time together. He'd let his feelings and his sex drive run away with him and now he had to suffer the consequences.

CHAPTER 18

DANTE

"Why the long face?" Linden dropped down next to Dante. He'd waited in the cafeteria, hoping Zane would drop by to see him before class, but Zane's class started ten minutes ago, and he hadn't shown. He'd try, the text said.

Zane had also blown him off the night before. And the night before. When Dante had managed to see him, he seemed weird and distant. Dante didn't want to push the issue with him, but only because he knew what was coming.

Zane didn't want to be with him anymore.

"I think Zane's going to dump me."

Linden frowned. "I'm sorry. Why? Did you guys fight?"

"No. Everything's been perfect. I know he only said he needed some extra study time before midterms, and I get it. This whole college thing fucking sucks, but... he made it bearable, you know."

"Boys are weird." Linden shrugged. "Can I do anything?"

"Nah. I need to wait it out, you know. See what's going on with him. Maybe he's just busy." Dante didn't believe his own words. Zane had already grown tired of him. Dante had been too clingy, too invested in what he thought was love, blossoming between them. Zane's sudden absence made Dante feel cold all over.

"You should come out with me tonight," Linden said. "We can go dancing."

"I need to study, but maybe after midterms?"

"I will make you."

Dante nodded. "Okay. After midterms." Dante's phone chimed and looked at the screen, hoping it was Zane. Maybe his class got bumped and he had time after all. Dante looked and his hopes crashed and burned when he saw it was an email from his mom.

"I have to meet my study group in five minutes. We're meeting on the second floor of the library if you want to join us."

Dante nodded. "Thanks. I'll think about it."

Once Linden left, Dante brought up the email his mom sent. He'd stretched the truth a bit when he talked to Jonathan or Zane. This was only the second time they'd had contact since he left for school.

The contents of the email were short and unsurprising in every way. She wasn't going to be home for Thanksgiving. She usually wasn't, and when she did make it. they marked the occasion with cheap turkey pot pies. But this year, she was going to Kentucky to spend Thanksgiving with her boyfriend's family. Dante didn't bother to reply.

The day only went downhill from there. He failed an assignment but managed to get a do-over from the professor. His cafeteria card got declined and his mom hadn't yet sent him the money she'd promised him so he could reload it. Dante's last class of the day let everyone go a few minutes early to try and beat the incoming storm, but the sky opened the minute Dante set foot outside. He trudged through the rain and by the time he got back to his building he was soaked through.

Dante shoved his way through the doors on the ground floor. He wiped the water off his face and attempted to dry his hand on his pants.

"Some weather we're having."

The sight of Zane in Dante's building sent hope coursing through him. Nothing mattered then. Not the approaching holiday. Not the failed paper. Not even Zane's constant brush offs or the bad weather mattered.

Dante stepped toward him and threw his arms around Zane. "Hey. I missed you."

He felt Zane's hand press against the small of his back. He felt the way Zane leaned in, pressed his face in the crook of Dante's neck and inhaled.

"How was your day?" Dante asked. "Are you coming up?" He hitched the strap of his bag higher on his shoulder.

Zane took a step back. He rubbed at the back of his neck with one hand and shoved the other in his front pocket.

"Yeah. But just for a minute." Zane stepped aside to let people pass. He wouldn't even look at Dante. He kept his gaze on the floor, the wall, anywhere but him.

Dante wanted to crawl in a hole. He'd been ready to give everything he had to Zane. All of him. His body. His soul. His heart. But none of it was good enough. Despite Zane's promise, he hadn't gotten tested. They hadn't had sex the way Dante had begged him to. And now Zane was here, in his building, in the rain, not looking at him.

"Well," Dante heard himself say. "What is it? If you're only coming up for a minute, we can talk right here. I won't keep you."

Zane looked at him then. He at least had the decency to look upset. "Dante, not here."

Dante shook his head. "Here's fine." He wouldn't cry in public, not with people milling about. But up in his room he'd fall apart. And he wouldn't do that in front of Zane. He didn't want his pity, or his sympathy. He didn't want his sadness or his regret.

"I like you, Dante. I like you too much."

Dante scoffed. "You like me so much I get the, it's not you it's me, line."

Zane looked struck, but Dante couldn't pull back his words. He knew what this was. He should've expected it from that first kiss. Dante was nothing more than a failed experiment. That's why Zane hadn't fucked him. He hadn't wanted to. His curiosity had been sated and now Dante would be set aside. Zane would find a nice girl and have his three point seven kids or whatever.

"Dante, this is my last year. I need to focus. I need to do better than I've been doing."

"I'm a distraction?"

Zane raked his fingers through his hair. "I'm fucking this up. Dante, I need time. Space. This year is huge for me. I don't want to hurt you."

Dante nodded. To his left, the elevator dinged, and the doors whooshed open. Dante waited for the three girls to step off. "I get it, Zane. It's fine. I'll see you around." Dante hurried into the elevator and pressed the button to close the doors.

"Dante, wait. Please." Zane's face disappeared as the doors slammed shut.

Dante trembled all the way up to the fourth floor, he practically ran to his room. He felt like a stupid kid. He should've stayed downstairs and let Zane tell him why he was the problem and not Dante, but it wouldn't have mattered because it was all lies.

He didn't think Zane had purposely hurt him, but the result was the same. Dante flung his door open and slammed it shut, he threw the lock and leaned against it and only then did he notice that Brant and Kim were in there.

Dante opened his mouth to say something, but suddenly Zane was there, knocking on his door.

"Dante, please. You don't get it. I said it all wrong. Come out and talk to me. Please."

Brant stood up and didn't bother with his discarded shirt. "Is he bothering you?"

Dante shook his head. His eyes burned with tears and his lip trembled. Kim stood and went to Brant. She put her hand on his shoulder. "I think Dante's being dumped."

Brant's eyes softened. "You want me to ask him to leave?"

Zane hadn't stopped begging the whole time and the sound of his voice was almost enough to break Dante's resolve. But he couldn't listen to anything Zane had to say. He didn't want to hear how he was a distraction, or that it wasn't his fault Zane had let himself get distracted. Either way, Zane wanted space. Space from him.

Dante looked at Brant and nodded. He stepped away from the door and went to the far corner of the room where Zane wouldn't be able to see him. Brant opened the door, but Dante watched the way he kept his body in the space.

"Dante would like you to leave." Brant said through gritted teeth. Dante flinched and hoped that Brant wouldn't hurt him.

He could hear Zane's ragged breathing. "Please, Dante. I didn't mean to hurt you."

Dante couldn't do it. He couldn't hide away in the corner while his roommate stood between them as a bodyguard.

He approached the door and Brant stepped aside. Dante looked at Zane.

"I know you didn't mean to hurt me." Zane reached for Dante, but he stepped back. "You still want space?"

"I need it, Dante. I need to focus on class."

"Okay. I understand. It's okay." It wasn't okay. "You took me by surprise is all. I'll... be fine."

"Dante," Zane's voice was filled with sympathy. He looked sorry. Like the night Dante had hurt himself on the stairs after trying to get to the roof. Rooftops were overrated, Dante had decided after that fiasco. Maybe love was, too.

"It's fine. What kind of friend would I be if I stood in the way of your education?"

Zane's face fell. "Friend?"

Dante held the door handle in a death grip. Right now, it was the only thing that kept him on his feet. "I'll always be your friend, Zane." Dante took a deep breath. "I need to change. I'm soaking wet. And then I need to study." Dante tried to keep his emotions at bay, but his lip trembled, and he knew Zane saw.

"Dante, babe, I'm sorry." Zane looked almost as wrecked as he felt, but Dante shook his head and closed the door. He engaged the lock then turned. He fell onto his bed and crammed his pillow in his mouth. Biting down kept him from screaming.

A weight came and settled on the edge of the bed and at first Dante didn't know what was going on, then a delicate hand, one too small to be Brant's, started rubbing circles on his back.

"I'm sorry, Dante," Kim said. "Is there anyone you want me to call?"

Dante shook his head and sniffled. Kim stood and left him, and he was vaguely aware of her and Brant whispering. Then, quietly, they left the room and Dante finally let go.

He cried as quiet as he could. He didn't want to alert the entire floor to the broken-hearted freshman. He felt like everybody would know. Like they'd whisper about the idiot who got dumped by the curious straight guy.

He'd mostly calmed down when Brant and Kim returned with two large pizzas, a box of wings, and a six pack of soda.

"We're watching bad horror movies." Brant said, setting the pizza on his desk.

"They're my favorite." Kim plopped down on the bed next to Dante and ran her fingers through his hair. "Come sit and eat with us. We'll watch some people get their guts torn out. It'll make you feel better." Kim frowned. "Well, okay, it won't, but it won't suck."

Dante could live with that. He forced himself to sit up, but he didn't want to sit on Brant's bed while he was still damp. He quickly changed his shirt and slid into a pair of cotton pajama pants before letting Kim tug him over to the bed. She sat in the middle and made Dante sit on her left. Brant sat on her other side and he queued a movie up on his laptop.

It was a horrible movie to end a horrible day, but Kim was right. It didn't suck. Now if only he could make the rest of his life not suck.

CHAPTER 19

ZANE

Zane knocked on Professor Thurston's door. His office hours were over ten minutes ago, but Zane had busted his ass to complete the assignment he missed. He'd barely slept in four days. Four long and torturous days where he thought of nothing but Dante or his stupid assignment.

"Come in." Thurston sounded annoyed and Zane hadn't even stepped foot in the office yet.

Zane entered. He wiped his clammy palm on his jeans. "Sorry if I'm interrupting." Zane glanced at Joe. It had been a huge source of gossip with Thurston's relationship with his men came out. No one really knew much of anything until he'd married Joe.

"What can I do for you? Make it short. We have dinner reservations." Thurston slid into his jacket and tossed some papers in his briefcase. "Joey, would you mind waiting outside?"

"It's okay, Professor. I wanted to ask if I handed in the assignment I missed right now, could I still get some sort of grade?"

Thurston raised his head and looked at the paper in Zane's hand. He could have submitted it via email, but he wanted to show the professor that he'd done it. He hoped it would sway the notoriously hard-assed professor's decision.

"You know I don't accept late assignments."

"I know, Professor. I'm sorry I missed it. I have no excuse, I hoped for a second chance. Even if you can't give me full marks."

Thurston looked like he was about to say something, then he glanced at Joe Carpenter. Former student of the university, and his husband. They had some sort of conversation where they didn't talk, but communicated telepathically, using eyebrows and intense gazes.

Thurston held out his hand. "Is that the paper?"

"Yes, sir." Zane handed it over and to his amazement, Thurston tossed it in his briefcase.

"You'll lose ten percent off the top and you'll never tell a soul about this extremely rare act of compassion. Now, if you'll excuse us." Thurston held his hand out and Joe took it. He tossed Zane a smile, then fell in next to Thurston. Zane would have to remember to send Joe a gift basket at Christmas.

Zane's victory felt hollow without Dante to celebrate with. Not that he had time to celebrate. Zane still had a mountain of work to do and he hadn't slept. It had been four days since he'd taken a knife to his own guts and shredded them.

Even if Zane had time to sleep, he couldn't. Every time he shut his eyes, he saw the way Dante's face fell. The way the light in his eyes died. The way he'd ran... from Zane. And Zane hated himself. He hated himself in the moment, but the words were out in the open and there was no taking them back.

"Hey, haven't seen you around in a while." Vanessa fell into step next to him. He was on his way to class.

"Been busy." Zane knew Vanessa would call him out. She'd make him talk and he didn't want to. The only person he wanted to talk to was Dante, but he was avoiding Zane. Zane's texts went unread. He tried calling but Dante never answered. It always went straight to voicemail.

"Noel told me what happened."

Zane grunted. Noel told her what he heard happened. Noel didn't have the whole story, no one did.

"Zane, talk to me." Vanessa put her hand on Zane's arm and pulled him to a stop. "Zane, you look like shit."

Zane laughed, but there was no heart in it. "Thanks. That makes me feel better."

"Why did you two break up? You're clearly not okay."

"Vanessa, I have class." Zane cut around her and went on his way. If he started talking, he'd crumble, and he couldn't afford it. He owed it to Dante to make the pain he put him through worth something. He couldn't toss everything aside now to wallow, or he'd have hurt them both for nothing. And Dante deserved more than that. Zane wanted to give him everything. He didn't know how he'd fallen that fast, but he had, and sometimes he wondered if fear of a different sort was what made him run.

"Zane, wait." Vanessa caught up to him. "You can talk to me."

"I know I can."

"You should talk to someone. If not me, then Noel or Ricky. Please. We're all worried about you."

"I'm fine."

"You look like shit. Dante does, too."

That made Zane stop. He turned to face Vanessa. "You've seen him?"

Vanessa bit at the pinky nail on her left hand, something she did when she was upset or nervous about something.

"When did you see him? How is he?"

Vanessa sighed. "You're both giant messes, okay? Is that what you want to hear? That he's just as miserable as you?"

Zane shook his head. "I never wanted to hurt him."

Vanessa forced a smile. She petted Zane's arm. "I know."

"I have class." Zane stepped back out of Vanessa's reach. "I can't be late."

"Talk to him, Zane."

Zane shook his head. "I've tried for four days. He won't talk to me."

"Try harder."

Zane nodded and turned. Class was the last place he wanted to be, but if it kept Vanessa away from him, it was probably for the best. Zane's wounds were raw, and Vanessa had marched up to him and rubbed salt in them as though he deserved it. And he did. He never should have kissed Dante. He never should have let himself get carried away. Until he got out of college and had a job, a steady income, a safety net, he had no business getting serious with someone. Right?

Zane hoped he'd done the right thing. With every day that passed, his resolve faded. His reasons seemed stupid, flimsy. An excuse.

Zane finally spotted Dante in the flesh during the week of midterms. Until now, Zane's schedule had been the same and Dante had been able to avoid him. They met outside the coffee shop, nearly crashing into each other.

Dante's friend Linden was with him and he tried to haul Dante away from Zane.

"Dante, please." Zane wasn't above begging. He'd been drowning without him and seeing him... it hurt. It hurt because he saw how much pain Dante was in and he'd caused it.

Dante nodded at Linden, who begrudgingly disappeared into the cafe.

"Dante, I'm sorry. I never meant to hurt you. You haven't checked any of my messages."

Dante shrugged, then hitched the strap of his backpack higher. "I've been busy."

Busy not taking care of himself. Zane was certain Dante had lost weight. The dark rings under his eyes told Zane he'd been sleeping about as well as Zane had.

Guilt and regret slammed him in the chest like a giant wielding a sledgehammer.

"I'm sorry. I missed an assignment and I panicked. I'm sorry."

Dante blinked at him, his expression remained flat and lifeless. "It's fine."

"It's not. I hurt you, Dante. I'm sorry." He couldn't tell Dante he missed him. He didn't want to hurt him more or lead him on. "Can't we talk? Be friends? Something."

Dante regarded him quietly for a few minutes. Then Linden returned with two coffees. He passed one to Dante. "Ready to go? Ansel's waiting on us."

"Ansel?"

"He's a friend." Dante paused and bit his lip. "I'll text you."

It was a small promise and it should've been a relief, but it wasn't. Zane watched Linden put his arm through Dante's and steer him away from Zane, back the way they came. It killed Zane to not know who Ansel was and why they were meeting. It killed him to be cut out of Dante's life. Breathing felt like his chest was filled with shards of glass and he was being cut to ribbons, like he'd slowly bleed out on the inside.

Zane watched them until they were out of sight, his gut tightening with every step Dante took away from him.

"Fuck." Zane shoved his hand in his pocket and discarded his untouched coffee in a nearby trash can. His stomach churned. He wanted to go after Dante and apologize, to beg his forgiveness. But he'd pushed him away. Because he was stupid and scared. Scared of one missed assignment.

"I'm an idiot." Zane said to himself as he finally made his feet move in the direction of his car. Back at home he couldn't even get himself to work on anything for school. He felt like a high school kid with a crush and a broken heart. Laying on his bed listening to love songs with his ear buds in, scrolling through photos of Dante didn't help either. Not that he had many to scroll through.

He'd taken one of Dante when he was sleeping. It had been one of the first nights he stayed over, one of the first nights they spent together. His face was soft and carefree. His pink lips slightly parted, Zane could still hear the gentle sound of him breathing.

Ricky knocked as he entered Zane's room. He grabbed the chair from Zane's desk and sat on it backward, his long arms folded over the back of the chair.

"Yes, I'm fine. No, I don't want to talk about it. Yes, I'm stupid. Yes, I've talked to him." Zane rolled his head to look at Ricky. "Happy?"

Ricky scoffed. "You have a one-track mind, my friend. That's your problem. I feel for your boy troubles, but I came in here because I have a hot job tip for you."

Zane sat up and tugged the earbuds from his ears. "Yeah?"

"My cousin, the one who works for his dad, well, he's getting married in June, and after they tie the knot, he's going to work in Uncle Greg's Los Angeles office. Which means Chad is getting a promotion, which means his position will be available. I took it upon myself to put a word in for you. My uncle knows you won't fully qualify until graduation, but he told me to tell you to apply."

Zane swung his legs off the side of the bed. "This is huge. This is unreal. Thanks, man."

Ricky shrugged. "It's not like I want to work with the family," he cringed. "No fucking thank you." Ricky pulled a slip of paper from his back pocket. "This is the email you need to send your application to."

Zane took the paper with trembling fingers. "Thanks."

Ricky slapped him on the back and left his room, pulling the door shut behind him. Zane appreciated his friends like Ricky, and he wouldn't squander the opportunity. Zane jumped up and turned his laptop on.

It took him a few minutes to spruce up his resume and send it off. Done, he pushed the chair away from the desk and sat there. He rubbed his hands down his face and exhaled a deep breath.

This was huge. It was everything he wanted, and it had been handed to him. It wasn't a guarantee, not yet, but Zane had hope. But he also had no one to share it with. He couldn't text Dante, not yet. He'd just seen him and understood they couldn't jump back into the easy friendship they'd had before Zane fucked everything up.

He hoped they'd get back there one day. Zane also wondered if friendship would be enough for him now that he knew the taste of Dante's lips. Since he'd slept tangled up with him, his bed seemed empty and cold in Dante's absence.

Zane moved back to his bed and flopped down on his back. He couldn't do this. He couldn't pretend he didn't want Dante back. But he'd blown it. Zane felt the familiar sting of tears. He sucked in a deep breath and let it out slowly.

He'd get Dante back. He'd beg if he had to. He'd give Dante everything he wanted. It wouldn't be easy, but he knew where to start. He checked the time and climbed out of bed. He splashed some water on his face, then drove to the campus health clinic.

On his list of fun things to do, spending time in waiting rooms sat at the bottom of the list, but Zane used his time wisely. Maybe it wasn't the greatest way to do it, but if he had any hope of getting Dante back, he couldn't be kept a secret. Not again. Dante deserved better than that. But he couldn't spring it on his family all at once. He'd come out first, then, when he got Dante back, he'd tell them right away.

Dante was worthy of being Zane's everything. He never should have stayed quiet about his sudden bisexual awakening, or his relationship with Dante. Looking back, there were a dozen things Zane did wrong. But he'd learn from his mistakes.

Zane rewrote the text about four thousand times before he sent it to Jonathan. In the end he laid it on the line.

Don't tell anyone, but I'm bisexual. Telling mom and dad later. Love you.

Jonathan's response was a whole line of eggplant emojis and a heart.

Love you bro

As the text came through, Zane got called to the back by a nurse. He tucked his phone away and followed her back. He'd back off if Dante told him there was no chance of them getting back together, but Zane wouldn't go to him empty handed. He'd have proof of how serious he was. He hoped he hadn't ruined things between them forever.

CHAPTER 20

DANTE

Dante walked into Casual Bottoms, Ansel's thrift store, with a knot of dread in his stomach.

"Relax, Dante. It's just dancing. You need a night out." Linden had been Dante's rock since the horrible split from Zane. Dante wasn't even sure he could say they'd broken up because he didn't know if they'd ever been together. Their relationship existed in a bubble and now it had burst.

Linden was determined to drag Dante out for a night of fun. Never mind that Dante didn't want to go. But moping in his dorm room hadn't done him any good.

Ansel came through the back and motioned at Linden. "Lock the door and flip the sign for me."

Dante had only briefly met Ansel once before when he came into the shop, but he seemed nice. He gave off a laid-back sort of vibe. Dante hoped Ansel was a wall hugger and he wouldn't be all alone at the club.

The sound of footsteps, heels on the hard floor approached from the back and a gorgeous man with long dark hair, tightly twisted into a braid which hung over his shoulder strutted through the beaded curtain. He wore shimmering tights, a low-cut tank, and bangles all up one arm.

"This is Brett." Linden had mentioned Brett and that they'd met here, but when pressed for more information, Linden clammed up. Dante suspected Linden had a crush on Brett, and who could blame him. Brett was gorgeous.

"I hope you don't mind me tagging along." Brett's voice was deep and sultry and not at all what Dante expected.

"Not at all." Linden said, slipping into an easy conversation with Ansel and Brett. The club they were going to let minors in, but didn't serve them alcohol, which Dante wasn't sure he wanted anyway. He'd barely been holding it together as it was.

Brett strutted over to Dante and admired the blue shirt Dante had put on. It hurt to put it on and go out somewhere Zane wouldn't be. There were memories attached to this particular shade of blue, but Dante should make new ones. Ones that didn't involve Zane.

Which had been the issue. Dante's whole life had instantly become Zane. Being around Zane was the point of waking up in the morning. The point of getting through class. The focus of his universe had narrowed to Zane's mouth the moment they'd kissed. Love was new for Dante, but he'd overdone it. He'd given too much of himself too fast.

"I love this color on you," Brett said. "I wish I looked half as good as you in this color."

"You probably look good in anything."

Brett's face lit up and he slid his slender arm around Dante's waist like they were old friends and hung out all the time. Dante didn't hate it. Sometimes he felt like a touch starved puppy and Brett's casual affection helped Dante relax.

"I like this one, we're keeping him."

Ansel shot Brett a look. "No more college kids in the basement. You were warned."

"You're no fun." Brett stuck his tongue out at Ansel. "Don't mind us, it's an inside joke about how I like to keep twinks in the basement."

Dante had heard the term before, but it had never been applied to him. "Twink? Me?"

Linden and Ansel laughed.

"Oh, you're precious. Of course, you're a twink. You're the best kind, too."

"I'm lost," Dante admitted.

"You're a sweet little snack. Like... something wholesome and organic. If you were a dessert, you'd be like... grandma's fresh apple pie."

"What would you be?" Dante asked.

Brett grinned. "One-hundred-percent Pop Tart. Compact, sweet, and totally bad for you. Now come one, if we leave now, we can get there before cover charge kicks in."

Dante was thankful that his mom, in a moment of guilt for bailing on Thanksgiving, had remembered to top up his bank account. One day he wouldn't have to rely on her or anyone else.

They took a cab to the club and slipped in as the place started to get busy. The music vibrated in Dante's chest. The club was dim, with the dance floor brightly lit. The DJ booth in the corner sat empty for the moment and some nameless dance track thumped through the space.

At the bar, Dante ordered a soft drink. The stamp on his hand prevented him from ordering anything with alcohol, but he noticed Ansel and Brett didn't share similar stamps.

"How old are you guys?" Dante asked, bringing his drink to his lips as they approached an empty table.

"Twenty-four, but don't worry, we were only joking about keeping twinks in the basement." Brett winked at Dante.

"Come dance with me." Brett tried to tug Dante out of his seat, but Dante stayed put.

"I'm not much of a dancer."

"You don't need to be."

Dante shook his head and Brett, thankfully, dropped the subject. He winked at Dante, for whatever reason, he didn't know, then stood and made his way down to the dance floor. Ansel joined him and Linden looked on longingly.

"Go ahead," Dante said.

"We came here to have fun, Dante." Linden pouted. "You can't tell me that you're going to have fun sitting alone in the booth all night."

Linden grabbed Dante's hand and wound their fingers together. "Dance with me then." Linden's round eyes plead with Dante. "Come on, Dante."

Dante sighed. "Fine."

He hadn't wanted to dance at all, but Linden turned out to be a great dance partner. Even though Dante had no idea what he was doing, Linden took the lead. He managed to keep enough space between them that Dante didn't feel as though he were being dry humped in public and it wasn't long before he worked up a sweat.

On a pause between songs, Linden leaned in. He pulled Dante into an awkward sort of hug from behind. His chin rested on Dante's shoulder and he held him loose around the waist.

"Admit it, you're not having an awful time."

Dante laughed. "I'm not hating it."

"Good. It's a start." Linden stepped back, putting a little space between them and they danced again.

Dante tried to keep his mind off Zane, but he wondered how it would feel if Zane were there dancing with him. How would Zane feel pressed up against Dante like a second skin, moving and sweating. He could almost feel the way Zane's cock would grind against his ass.

Dante stepped away from Linden, painfully aware he'd never get to experience that with Zane now. He'd never get a lot of things with Zane, but that didn't mean he couldn't have them with anyone.

"I need to piss. I'll be right back." Dante made a beeline for the bathroom. He took a quick leak and washed his hands. A glance in the mirror proved that Brett had been right. He looked good in this shade of blue.

Dante left the bathroom and this time when he hit the dance floor again, he didn't flinch when Linden danced a little closer. He let himself melt into the music, let it carry him away to a place where the only thing that existed was the constant throng of a baseline and the burning arousal in his gut.

The swell of arousal slowed him down. His heart was still attached to Zane, and arousal caused by someone else, by something else, felt wrong in a way Dante couldn't describe.

And it made him angry. Zane had made him feel like this. Why did he let Zane have this control over him now that they weren't together? It wasn't fair that Dante was out having a good time and the shadow of Zane followed him, haunted him, robbed him of the fleeting joy he'd felt on the dance floor.

Dante's burgeoning erection flagged, taking with it his enthusiasm for dancing. Dante shrugged out of Linden's touch and motioned to the bar.

"I'm getting tired. I think I'll sit a few songs out."

Linden gave Dante a thin-lipped smile and nodded. To his surprise, Brett followed him up to the bar. Brett copied Dante's order of a lemon-lime soda. They found an empty table and slid into seats opposite each other.

Out on the dance floor, Linden and Ansel had found each other and were wrapped up in a dance far too hot for Dante to watch. It made him feel like a peeping tom. He turned his attention to Brett instead.

"If you were having fun out there, you didn't need to stop. I'm okay by myself."

Brett laughed. "You say that now, but you're shark bait, baby boy."

"Please don't call me that." Dante wrinkled his nose.

"Sorry, but I feel like I have to protect you. There's guys here who can smell blood in the water a mile away and you've been bleeding out all night long. Sweet young thing like you, nursing a broken heart, that's easy prey to some of these guys."

Dante scoffed. "They can try, but the only place I'm going after this is my dorm. Alone." By the way Brett talked, it made him think Linden might have told him or Ansel about his recent heartbreak. "Did Linden tell you about my breakup?"

Brett shook his head. "But if you've seen one kicked puppy, you've seen them all, and you had the look of someone who has recently spent a lot of time feeling kicked."

Dante took a sip of his drink. He stared at his glass and the rivulets of condensation built up on the outside. He didn't see the implication that Zane had kicked him. Dante had been an experiment, or something. A lapse in judgement. A mistake. But Dante knew Zane never meant to hurt him. Of everything that happened, it was the only thing Dante was still sure about. That, and the fact that he was still six-thousand percent in love with Zane.

"For the record," Dante said. "I'm not a kicked puppy."

Brett smiled and nodded. "Okay, but I'm still going to sit over here with you because no one in here tonight is interesting."

"What do you find interesting?" Dante asked.

Brett sighed and propped his head on his hand. His manicured nails lay against his cheek, the white polish gleamed even in the low light of the club.

"I like guys who look like me," Brett confessed. His eyes were filled with a far-off wistful look. "But most guys who look like me want guys who don't look like me. I want someone who I can share all of me with. My nail polish collection. My wigs. My clothes. I want to find someone who gets all of me, without me having to explain things to them about why I am how I am and like what I like."

"I get it." Dante took a drink to wet his parched throat. He'd had that with Zane. As brief and fleeting as it had been, he'd had that. Zane knew him. Maybe not every bit of him, but enough that Dante never worried about how to act around him. About what to say or if he was too quiet, or not quiet enough. Dante wasn't a very interesting person, he knew this about himself. But Zane had made him feel like he was.

"Hey, you okay?" Brett asked. His brow pinched in concern.

"I... I think I've danced enough for one night."

Brett nodded. "I'll go get the boys. We can head back to the store and hang out where it's quieter and not as sweaty."

Dante nodded. In fact, he wanted to be anywhere but here, but most of all, he wanted to be with Zane. But that wasn't going to happen. He could wallow alone in his dorm, like he'd been doing. Or he could spend a few more hours pretending he wasn't dying on the inside, but at least he wouldn't be alone.

"Mom, I'm bisexual." Zane's dad had gotten called into work at the last minute and wasn't able to make the call, but after telling them that he had something important to share with them, Zane could hardly bow out and wait for his dad to be available.

Zane watched his mom's expression flicker for a moment before she plastered on a big, and completely genuine smile. "Do you have a boyfriend, then?"

"Not right now." Zane admitted. He should have told her and dad back when he first thought of Dante as someone he could love. There had been no reason for him to keep his newfound sexuality a secret. Except fear.

He wasn't afraid she'd reject him. His parents were the epitome of cool. They'd always believed in things like equal rights and gay marriage. They'd accepted Dante without question. Zane should have told them. Far too late to go back and fix the mistakes he made, he'd prevent himself from making the same ones.

"There was a boy then?" Zane's mom practically swooned.

"There was. I hope there will be again. He was... he was special."

"Oh, baby. Tell me all about him."

Zane shook his head. "I can't. I made a mess of things. I hurt him. I... I did a lot of things wrong. In other news, though," Zane desperately needed to change the subject before he spilled his guts. "Ricky's uncle might have an opening for me after graduation. I'd start right out of college."

"Oh baby! I'm so happy for you. That's amazing."

"It's not a sure thing, yet."

"I'm proud of you. You've worked so hard."

It was hard to feel good about the praise when it came with the guilt attached. He'd hurt Dante because his focus slipped, and he panicked. "Thanks, mom."

"Well, that was unenthusiastic."

"Sorry. I've got a lot on my mind, that's all. Are you ready for Thanksgiving?"

"Your dad bought the turkey the other day. It's a big one. Even though Jonathan won't be here, I can send the leftovers back with you and Dante."

Zane hadn't forgotten Dante would be joining them for Thanksgiving. It was part of his plan to win him back. Zane had his test results back, he'd come out to his brother, and his parents. He had some things to iron out before he got the ball rolling, but he was determined to win Dante back.

"I have to run, Mom." Zane glanced at the clock. Dante would be leaving class soon and Zane planned to put his plan into motion. He'd made Dante run from him twice now. First, after the kiss. Then again when he broke his heart. He had a lot to make up for but proving Dante hadn't lost his friendship would be a good start.

"Oh? Somewhere more important to be?"

Zane grinned. "You could say that. I have a boy to win back."

"Good luck, Sweetheart." Zane could tell by the look on her face that she wanted to say more. That if he let her start, she'd blather for days about how great he was, and as much as he welcomed the motherly love, he had a heart to unbreak.

"Love you Mom. Talk soon."

"Bye."

Zane gave himself a cursory check to make sure he looked good before he hurried to Dante's classroom. Even if Zane hadn't been head over heels for Dante, he'd still missed his presence.

Zane stood in the hallway and waited and a few seconds after the hour, a line of students poured out of the room. Zane fell into step beside Dante, who did a double take.

"Hey," Zane said. He felt oh-so-smooth in that moment. He'd had so much time to think of what to say to Dante and *hey* was the best his stupid brain came up with.

"Hey," Dante returned Zane's greeting without enthusiasm. He seemed guarded, and Zane hated what he caused. Dante hadn't run yet, and he'd take that as progress.

"Do you want to grab a coffee?"

Dante shook his head. "Can't. I bombed a midterm and I need to study my ass off."

"What subject?"

"Math. It's always fucking math."

"Study with me." Zane blurted. "I mean, I'll help if you want. We can sit in the library or the cafe. We can still have coffee, if you want. Tutoring services on the side. No charge."

Dante shrugged. "I don't know."

"Let me help you. Please."

"What about your own studies?" Dante asked. His voice

had a little bite to it, like he wanted to be angry with Zane, but didn't know how.

"I'm caught up." Zane stopped. He grabbed Dante's arm and turned to face him. "I never should have said any of that. I freaked out because I missed an assignment, which I've never done. It got to me in a way I didn't expect, and I panicked."

Dante nodded. "I get it." His flat voice sounded unconvinced, then he sighed. "You were right, though. It was too much, too fast. We jumped in with both feet and I think we got a little ahead of ourselves. I could use some help... from a friend."

Zane had a long road ahead of him to earn Dante's heart. For now, he'd take every scrap of Dante he could get. He would prove he could be everything Dante wanted, and deserved to have.

Zane swallowed all the things he wanted to say and nodded. "I'll always be your friend, Dante." The words were ash on his tongue. They weren't the declaration he wanted to make, but he broke something between them when he pushed Dante away.

They set up in the library. Neutral ground should have made it less awkward for them, but they still stumbled through their conversation like they were navigating a rocky hiking trail in the dark.

"What problems are you having with the material?" Zane asked, pulling up a chair next to Dante.

Dante sighed and rummaged in his bag, pulling out his textbook. "I thought I understood the material. But the grade I got indicated I don't." Dante set his math text on the table and glared at it. "I don't even know what I want to do with my life, but I know I don't want it to be anything that makes me do this shit."

Zane hid a smile. Dante's distress shouldn't be cute, but the little rant gave him a flicker of hope that things could return to normal between them. Eventually. Because even now the awkwardness ebbed back in like a tide of suck. Dante cleared his throat and flipped the book open.

"I completely bombed."

"Well, let's start at the beginning." Zane flipped the book open to the first chapter. Any thought that Dante might have failed because his mind was elsewhere during midterms went out the window when they started working. After a few practice questions, it became clear to Zane that Dante should have sought help a while ago.

"Why didn't you say you were having this much trouble?" Zane whispered. "How did you manage last year?"

Dante shrugged and started another question. Zane couldn't tell if his determination was to get it right, or to simply prevent himself from going into Hulk-mode and tearing the textbook in half.

"Jonathan was in class with me." Dante frowned. "It's not fair you know. He's a math genius and a super talented artist. Aren't you only supposed to be good at one or the other?"

"I'm not sure there's rules to any of this, but if I can't help you, Noel probably could. He's like... my Jonathan. Anything I can do, he can do better. I won't let you fail, Dante."

Dante glanced at him from the corner of his eye. "Don't make promises you can't keep." The venom in Dante's voice shot one-hundred proof misery straight into Zane's blood stream. For a minute he couldn't think. Dante's words had wiped his mind of everything but the knowledge that he'd done this. He was the reason for Dante's unhappiness, and it nearly killed him.

Zane cleared his throat and shifted in his seat. "Let's try this again." He wouldn't pretend Dante hadn't said anything, but for now he'd pretend he wasn't bleeding out on the inside. Dante wanted his friendship, and Zane could give it to him without the burden of censoring himself to manage Zane's emotions. Zane could handle a few hurt feelings. He had it coming.

They spent the next hour working in hushed whispers. They discussed nothing but numbers and though it was awkward from first to last, it was a step up from the way things had been between them, which had been nonexistent.

"You're going to be late for class," Dante reminded Zane. He flipped his books closed.

Zane glanced at his watch. He had fifteen minutes before his class started, but he wasn't ready to leave Dante yet. The idea that he could miss class to stay with Dante longer floated through his brain and he quickly quashed it. It was his addiction to Dante that had started this whole mess.

"I'll text you to set up more times for tutoring."

Dante nodded and quietly packed his gear away. "Yeah. Thanks. It was nice of you to help today."

"I was happy to help." Zane looked at the time again. "I have to get going."

"I know." Dante bit his lower lip. Once upon a time he could've leaned in and kissed Dante goodbye. He missed that mouth. That person. Dante had sat beside him for over an hour, but it hadn't been the version of Dante he was used to. This had been the monochrome Dante in place of the technicolor one.

"See you later."

Dante nodded and zipped his bag before sliding it over his shoulder. "Yeah. See you."

Zane didn't move from his spot until Dante was long gone.

CHAPTER 22

DANTE

Linden's weight next to Dante was comforting, grounding, and temporary. Linden stretched and yawned. They hadn't meant to fall asleep, but their late-night study session had turned into a sleep over.

"Are you sure you don't want to come home with me for Thanksgiving? My dad won't mind. He might force feed you his homemade cranberry sauce, then make you tell him that it's better than store bought, but he's mostly harmless."

"Mostly harmless?"

"Mostly. He takes food very seriously. You might slip into a food coma, but other than that, you won't be harmed."

Dante laughed. "I'll be fine."

"You're going to go home then? With him?" Linden threw his arm around Dante and burrowed in closer. "Is that smart?"

"It's what I always do."

"You're not just saying you're going with Zane so you can tell him you're going with me so you can secretly be here all alone for Thanksgiving, are you?"

"You're insane. Zane's mom makes the best pumpkin pie. The awkward car ride is worth it."

"Shit, maybe I'll come home with you then. I can keep you away from Zane and gorge myself on pie. It's a win-win."

Dante wrinkled his nose. "You can stop being mad at him, you know."

Linden laughed. "Never. It's the code of the best friend. He fucking stomped on you and I will die mad about it."

Dante laughed at the possessive way Linden hugged him. It made Dante think of him like an angry starfish. "I'll be fine. Zane and I were friends before all this, and we'll be friends again."

"I thought you were friends now?" Linden sat up and stared down at Dante.

"We're... trying? It's been weird between us. I keep waiting for things to go back to normal, but there's always this..."

"Gigantic elephant of sexual tension in the room?"

Dante shook his head. "Zane doesn't want me like that. Mostly I think it's his regret."

"His regret? Don't you have any?"

"When it comes to Zane? No. I can't regret it, even though I got hurt." Dante shrugged. It probably made him eight different kinds of pathetic, but his pain had been a drop in the bucket compared to the ocean of pleasure he'd lived belonging to Zane, even though it had been fleeting.

"If I find someone to love me half as much as you love him, I'm not going to be an idiot like Zane was."

Dante sniffed. "Thanks."

"Are you sure you don't want to ditch him and come home with me? I know Jonathan isn't going to be there to buffer for the two of you."

"I'll be fine."

"I have to pack and get on the road, but text me if you need me. I'll pretend to have an emergency. A big one. It'll be bad and you'll have to rush to my side." Linden stood and stretched before stuffing his books into his bag. They'd spent the night before going over the math he'd been working on with Zane over the past few weeks.

"You worry too much." Dante climbed out of bed. He had time to pack and have a quick shower, but only if he hurried Linden out of his dorm room. "I'll be okay. I promise." Dante ushered Linden to the door. "Now go so I can shower."

"I could help." Linden waggled his eyebrows at Dante.

"Not a chance."

"You're a spoil sport."

"Have a good holiday."

"You too." Linden clapped him on the shoulder then he was gone. To keep his mind occupied, Dante packed for the weekend then had a quick shower. It was quiet in the building as a lot of the student population had left the day before. Linden hadn't been totally off base. Dante had pondered skipping Thanksgiving altogether. He could've opted to stay on campus. Alone.

Dante wasn't a glutton for punishment. He didn't want to stay at school all by himself. His mom might not have cared enough to stick around to see him, but it didn't mean Dante had to be completely alone. He might not be with Zane anymore, but he still loved Zane. He loved Zane's parents like they were his own. And even though Jonathan was still in Los Angeles, he'd be there in spirit.

Zane texted Dante that he was on his way. Dante grabbed his bag and headed down the stairs and out into the crisp November morning. They didn't get a lot of snow around here. If they did, it came in January or February and only stayed long enough to be inconvenient to everyone. But today the clouds hung low and fat. The sky looked dark and ominous. Dante set his bag down and zipped his jacket.

Zane pulled up a moment later. He leaned across the front seat and popped the passenger side door open for Dante.

Dante flung his bag over the seat into the back then climbed in. Zane's car smelled like him. Like cologne, like Zane and Dante fought back the urge to climb across the seat and bury his face against Zane's chest. He wanted to soak up every bit of the aroma until it leaked out of his pores.

"Hey," Dante said, feeling absolutely awkward. The next four hours would be a lesson in torture.

"Hey."

Unless Dante was mistaken, Zane's gaze raked over his body, checking him out.

"Hey," Dante repeated like an idiot, but Zane only smiled.

"Do you want to stop to eat or grab something from a drive thru? Mom can sense a missed meal a mile away."

Dante groaned. It was true, and a little heart-warming. "Let's get drive thru."

"Breakfast sandwiches?"

"Yes." Dante snapped his seatbelt into place. "Sausage. Three of them. And a coffee."

"Their coffee is like roofing tar. We'll stop at Starbucks for the good shit and get the breakfast sandwiches after."

Dante settled into his seat. They didn't talk much until they were on the road, their half drank coffees cooling in the cup holders and their stomachs full of the greasiest, most wonderful breakfast Dante had eaten in ages.

Maybe time healed some wounds, because Dante didn't ache the way he used to when Zane had first split up with him. Maybe time would make things less awkward between them. Maybe one day, Dante would find someone to fall in love with and maybe he wouldn't fuck it up.

Still, having Zane close these past few weeks had been an exercise in torture. The hours they spent huddled together at the library had sent Dante home half hard and desperate for release more often than not. Zane had been a perfect gentleman; he'd been a good friend. He sat with Dante and worked on his assignments while Dante struggled with his math.

Through it all, Dante never stopped wanting him. He wished things could've turned out different than they had, but maybe time would heal that wound, too.

"You're quiet," Zane said. "You okay?"

Dante glanced at him and shrugged. "I'm fine. Tired, I think. I was up late studying with Linden."

"How's the math coming?"

Dante groaned. "I hate it. I hate it with the fire of a thousand suns. And part of me understands why freshman must take a bunch of different bullshit courses, but part of me is kicking and screaming because I never want to look at another algebra equation as long as I fucking live."

Zane laughed. He opened his mouth like he wanted to say something, then he closed his mouth and stared at the road.

Dante turned his attention back to the scenery flying past. The world wasn't as green in November. Everything was muted and dull. Like Dante's whole life had been. Until Zane. Zane had lit up his world. He'd breathed life and color into Dante's universe, and now Dante was trapped in an endless November.

Maybe he wasn't as over Zane as he'd thought he was. He knew he wasn't. But he wanted to be. If he couldn't be with him, then he wanted to be Zane's friend. But just friends felt impossible. He couldn't count the times he had to stop himself from touching Zane. Friends might touch, but Zane and Dante hadn't been the kinds of friends who touched.

Touch between them had meant something more. It hadn't been casual. Not from the first kiss. Everything from that moment on had been the most serious, most important thing in Dante's life.

And now he had to somehow get used to this old normal. This old camaraderie that should be easy to slip back into but felt like a sweater stretched in the wash. It didn't fit anymore.

They stopped for gas and to stretch their legs halfway there, but Dante thought it was an excuse for Zane to get away from him and out of the awkwardness for a few minutes. Every one of their attempts to have a conversation ended with someone not saying something. Dante's feet hurt from the eggshells he walked on around Zane, but he didn't know how to stop.

Arriving back home was weird. Nothing had changed while Dante had been away but coming back felt different.

"Are you staying with your mom?" Zane asked, exiting the freeway.

"She's in Kentucky with her new boyfriend."

Zane's head snapped to the side and he looked at Dante, slack jawed. His mouth closed and anger sparked in his eyes. "I try to keep my opinion to myself, because she's your mom, but I fucking hate her."

Zane's anger on his behalf loosened something inside Dante and he laughed. It surprised them both. Zane looked at him like he'd grown a second head, but Dante couldn't stop. He loved Zane for hating his mom. Dante couldn't. She was his Mom. She wasn't perfect, or there, or anything most of the time, but she was still all he had.

The corner of his life she occupied had steadily shrank the older Dante got. The more he was able to take care of himself, the more he had to. And now, because he didn't need her, she'd made the decision that she didn't have to be around at all. It sometimes occurred to Dante to be mad about it, but mostly he didn't let himself think about it too much. Focusing on the things he'd never have was a depressing exercise in futility. Wishes never came true. They weren't like goals. They weren't something he could plan to achieve. Wishing his mother gave a shit had never given him anything but a broken heart.

Zane's house came into view a few minutes later. Dante could tell from the rigid way Zane held himself he was still mad about Dante's mom. Dante thought his anger was sweet, but unnecessary. After all, pulling into Zane's driveway felt like coming home. Dante knew the only feeling his mom's house would give him would be emptiness.

Maybe it was good he and Zane had parted before they'd done permanent damage to their friendship. If things had been ugly between them, Dante would lose all this. Across town his own house sat vacant.

This was the only family he had.

Dante climbed out of the car and grabbed his bag from the back seat. Four hours of awkwardness paid off when the door opened, and Zane's mom beamed at them both with her wide, sunny smile. She was like Jonathan, Dante noticed with a pang. He missed his best friend. He missed Zane. He'd missed their parents. Dante didn't often let her fuss over him, or he pretended to not want her to, but when she wrapped her arms around Dante and pulled him into a hug, he went willingly.

"I missed you," she said, giving him a final squeeze before she released him. "And you're so skinny. Come on, I'll make you boys lunch."

Dante closed the door. November wasn't totally bleak after all.

CHAPTER 23

ZANE

Lunch was Dante's favorite. Zane loved that his mom fussed over Dante. She always had. It was partly because that's who she was. She donated her time to charities. She babysat the neighbor kids for free, she rescued stray cats, and she fussed over Dante.

Dante dipped the corner of his grilled cheese sandwich into the tomato soup and smiled as he took a bite. "I swear this is the best thing I've eaten since I left, Claire."

She walked past, ruffling her fingers through Dante's hair. She was the kind of mom Dante deserved to have. Someone soft and kind. Someone who gave a shit. Who wouldn't abandon their kid.

"I know tomato soup isn't your favorite, Zane, but you don't need to scowl," his mom said.

"I wasn't scowling at the soup. It was a general scowl."

"Everything okay?"

"Everything's fine." Zane stuffed his mouth full of sandwich. "Where's dad?" Zane asked once he swallowed.

"Your father is dead. I buried him in the backyard."

"Uh oh." Dante said, not hiding his grin. "What did he do this time?"

Zane's mom twisted the dish towel in her hands. "He wanted to deep fry the turkey."

Dante frowned. "But how do you get stuffing if you deep fry the turkey?"

"Exactly!" His mom exclaimed. "He made a trip to the grocery store. He'll be back in a bit. What do you two have planned?"

Dante shrugged. "I'll probably study math, then facetime Jonathan and mock him for missing out on turkey tomorrow."

"Don't you get enough studying at school? This is supposed to be a holiday. Do holiday things." Zane's mom topped up her coffee. "Go for a drive, see some friends. Don't spend your whole weekend staring at math problems. They'll be there later."

Dante groaned. "That's the problem."

"That place in the mall that sells the frosted malts is closing after Christmas." Zane's mom said. "You should go spoil your dinner."

"We just ate lunch." Zane took his dirty dishes and loaded them into the dishwasher.

His mom rolled her eyes. "You're perpetually hungry. The two of you are stomachs with legs. Go get a malt before they're gone forever."

"Okay, you win. We'll go get malts. If I didn't know better, I'd think you were trying to get rid of us."

"This is your last Thanksgiving break. After this, you'll be out in the world with your job and you might not have time to get a frosted malt."

"Ah, this is some sort of seize the day thing." Zane fished his keys out of his pocket and headed for the door. Dante loaded his dishes into the dishwasher and followed him.

They said a quick goodbye to Zane's mom. Once they were outside, Dante laughed.

"Do you think she could've tried any harder to get rid of us?"

"She's never cared so much about a frosted malt before. I want to say something's up, but we both know mom. She gets nostalgic over the weirdest things. She probably has a nice memory of taking us all for frosted malts one time ten years ago and is sad that it's closing or something. She's weird."

Dante shrugged. "She's great. At least she gives a shit."

Zane winced. "Sorry."

"Nothing you can do."

"Is there a reason why your mom is an ice queen?"

They rode in silence to the mall, but eventually, Dante answered Zane's question. "I wasn't exactly planned. Mom was in her last semester of high school when she got pregnant. She couldn't get an abortion and my dad bailed on her. I don't think she wanted me very much. She doesn't talk about her parents, they died when I was a kid, but she doesn't seem to miss them."

Zane exhaled. "Shit. That sucks."

"It is what it is." Dante shoved his hands in his pockets or Zane might have grabbed one. He wanted Dante back. He wanted to be the caring boyfriend who held Dante while he poured his heart out. Realistically, he knew he couldn't kiss everything better, but he wanted to try.

Dante deserved far more than he was given. Zane wanted to shower him with love and affection. He wanted to fill his life with laughter and happiness. He wanted to be Dante's safe space. He wanted to provide and protect. All the ways Zane had fucked up suddenly felt like they were too much for him to expect Dante to get over.

His own mother had pushed him away his entire life. She'd all but abandoned him. And Zane had pushed him away. At the time it had seemed like the only option, but it was one of those things Zane would regret forever.

Zane ordered two frosted malts. He handed one to Dante and shook his head at the sight of the wallet in Dante's hand. "Put your money away. It's my treat."

"Are you sure?"

"Let me treat you, Dante. Please."

Dante put his wallet away.

"What are your plans after graduation? You have to be excited."

"It doesn't seem real yet. I still have one more semester after this, but it's so close I can taste it. Ricky's uncle has a job ready for me when I graduate, which is huge."

"Must be nice to have that kind of solid plan for your future. I don't even know what I'll pick for a major."

"You have time."

Dante shrugged.

"You can talk to me, you know."

Dante sighed. "I hate college. Well, not really. I hate not having a plan. A direction. Everything feels so big, you know." Dante stabbed his spoon into his malt. Watching Dante eat got Zane all kinds of hot. He imagined all the ways Dante's tongue would make him feel if it were on his skin.

"You don't have to do any of this alone. You have Jonathan, and Linden, and my parents, and me." Especially me. Always me.

Dante looked at him and the sheen in his eyes gave Zane a lump in his throat. Before Zane had a chance to confess his feelings in the middle of a crowded mall, Dante looked at him again.

"Would you mind if we stopped by my house? I want to get a few things from my room."

"Yeah. No problem." Zane didn't want to talk about Dante's

mom, or her reasons for not being there for him. The fact was if Zane ever came face to face with the woman, he'd probably tear into her, no matter how Dante felt about it.

Dante lived in a townhouse a few minutes away from the mall. The long strip of joined houses came into view and Zane frowned at what he saw.

"Dante? Did you know?"

"That she was selling the house?" Dante's laugh was tight and miserable. "I guess I missed the memo."

Zane slowed the car. "We don't have to do this right now if you don't want to. We can come back later."

Dante shook his head. "There might not be a later. Help me with my stuff?"

"Yeah." Zane pulled into the driveway and they got out of the car. Dante stared up at the house for a minute before producing his key and unlocking the front door.

The house was immaculate. Free of clutter and dust, it looked ready to sell. Dante left his shoes on and climbed the stairs to his bedroom.

"At least she didn't throw my stuff away." Dante opened his closet and took the remaining clothes out, hanger and all, and laid them on the bed. "Can you grab my books? Toss them in the laundry basket."

Zane did as Dante asked. They worked quietly, emptying the last of Dante's belongings and loading them into the car didn't take long.

"Think Jonathan will mind if I stuff this shit in his room? It's not like he's there anyway."

"You can keep it in mine. I don't mind."

"Right," Dante nodded. "Not like you're going to be around much longer anyway, right."

"Dante," Zane's voice trembled. He'd wanted more time to approach Dante about everything. He wanted to wait until there was a good moment. A moment when things were perfect for Zane to lay it all on the line. To confess how much he loved Dante and that he'd been miserable without him. But perfect moments didn't happen that way.

Zane stepped in Dante's way before he could leave the room.

"Dante, wait. I'll always be there for you."

Disbelief stared back at Zane and he swallowed. He took the box from Dante and set it off to the side.

"From the moment I hurt you, I knew I'd made a mistake. I panicked. It wasn't just about the assignment. It was..." Zane paused and took a breath. His hands twitched with the need to touch Dante, but he couldn't, not yet. "I regret hurting you, Dante. More than anything."

Dante's face fell and Zane closed the distance. He captured Dante's face in his hands. His thumbs followed the slope of Dante's cheekbones. "Not you, babe. I never regretted you. I should have told my parents sooner. I should have been a grown up and had a conversation with you about my schoolwork and my missed assignment. I shouldn't have pushed you away. I did a lot of things wrong, and I don't blame you if you never forgive me, but Dante, you have to know I don't regret you. Never."

Zane leaned in and pressed his lips to Dante's. They trembled beneath his touch, and Dante's hands came up and gripped Zane's biceps. The tips of his fingers dug into the flesh, almost to the point of pain. Dante's eyes sparkled with terror and hope.

"You don't... you're not sorry... about us?"

Zane kissed him again. Softer. Because he could. Because he wanted to wrap Dante in softness and security. "I'm only sorry that I hurt you. I'm sorry, Dante. More sorry than you'll ever know."

Dante's lip trembled, and Zane kissed him. Dante moaned into Zane's mouth. It was half-whimper, half desperate plea. As much as Zane wanted to do nothing but kiss him, they had to talk first. Dante had to know that this was it for Zane.

Zane pulled away. "I want you back, Dante."

Dante nodded.

"No more running from me." Zane slid his hands down Dante's sides. Dante settled in closer. "I mean it, Dante. From now on, we're in this together."

"No more running." Dante made a cross over his heart. "And you, no more breaking up with me."

"Deal." Zane pecked him on the lips. "You know, I expected you to make me grovel a lot more than this."

"I'm not one to look a gift horse in the mouth. You said you're sorry and I believe you."

"I'm going to spend the rest of my life making that up to you."

Dante shifted closer, pressing the evidence of his arousal into Zane's leg. "Tell you what." The gentle way he caressed Zane's neck made him shiver. "Kiss me, touch me, be with me, right here, and we'll call it even."

Zane laughed, but he couldn't resist Dante's sweet bargain. He wove his fingers through Dante's hair and pulled him into a kiss. Hard and deep. He backed Dante up until his legs hit the bed and when he went down, Zane followed.

CHAPTER 24

DANTE

Zane's weight comforted Dante. It made him believe this was real, that this was more than a fleeting echo of happiness, bouncing off his empty chest and reverberating into an empty eternity.

Dante gripped Zane, unwilling to let him go, even to get their clothes off. They kissed like their lives depended on it. Maybe they did. Because Dante felt dead without him. Even his friendship had been a pale replacement for the warmth Zane brought to his life.

Zane ground against him, lighting him up. Every point of contact burned with heat and electricity. Dante kissed the corner of Zane's mouth. Zane latched onto his neck, sucking a hickey up to the surface of his skin.

Dante's head spun. But he wanted this. "Zane, please." He didn't even know what he was begging for.

"I got you." Zane's breath was hot in Dante's ear. His hands moved with purpose, with certainty. He sat up on his knees and dragged his hands down Dante's torso. Dante shivered when Zane's hands pushed his shirt up out of the way. Wet heat captured Dante's nipple and he arched off the bed.

Zane chuckled against Dante's skin. He wove his fingers through Zane's hair. He liked that he could touch him again the way he wanted. He wanted to feel all of Zane. Every bit of him. He knew they wouldn't get there today, at least not right now, but the slide of Zane's tongue, tickling down the center of Dante's chest was enough.

Dante hissed when Zane kissed his stomach, below his belly button, right above his zipper. Zane's hands blazed trails of heat down Dante's body. He shook when Zane's mouth closed over Dante's erection. Through jeans and briefs, it didn't matter. It was the hottest moment in his life.

Zane looked up at him. His gaze flickered with raw vulnerability. "I've never done this before."

"Neither have I." Dante didn't laugh at their mutual awkwardness. He pushed a lock of hair off Zane's forehead. Zane closed his eyes and kissed Dante's stomach again. His zipper slid down, the metal teeth separating one by one. Dante felt each one let go like an inhibition vanishing, being dissolved by starry-eyed bravery.

Zane's mouth closed over the head of Dante's cock. This time through briefs. He pulled away too soon and Dante whimpered.

"Patience." Zane hooked his fingers into the sides of Dante's pants. He pulled down and Dante lifted his ass to make it easier for him. Dante's cock sprang free and bobbed up in the air. Precum beaded on the head and he watched Zane's gaze flicker to it. Then he locked eyes with Dante and leaned in. He swiped his tongue over the head, gathering the bead of moisture onto his tongue.

This moment felt like a ray of sunlight. It was something he could see. He could feel. But he couldn't keep. There'd be other moments like it though, and that warmed Dante like the sun.

He wouldn't run. Not again. And if Zane tried to push him

away, he wouldn't go. Dante shook, dangerously close to coming, even though Zane had just started. "Slow down," his voice shook as he begged.

"It's okay if you come." The look in Zane's eyes was marked mischief. "I want you to feel good. Besides," Zane licked a trail up the underside of Dante's cock. "Maybe I want to see how fast I can make you come."

Dante laughed, weak and breathy. "I've come in my head about three and a half times already."

"Half an orgasm? That's talent." Zane took the head of Dante's cock into his mouth and swirled his tongue over the tip. Dante's body took on a mind of its own. His shoulders pressed into the mattress and his hips came off the bed. He didn't come, but it was a near thing. His orgasm came to the edge, then ebbed away.

Zane's hands caressed Dante's body. They traveled over his skin in languid strokes, up his sides and across his stomach. Zane wrapped one hand around the base of Dante's cock.

Dante had never known this sort of pleasure before. Even the other times he'd been with Zane didn't compare. The difference was the way he felt when Zane looked at him now, when he touched him, when his eyes closed and his lashes fanned against his cheeks, Dante could feel how much Zane cared for him. Or maybe he felt how much he cared about Zane. The difference was that before their explorations had been heady and explosive. The world still existed beyond them, but it was this intangible idea, because the idea of anything existing beyond them wasn't a concept Dante could grasp as Zane made love to him with his mouth. His hands. His breath. Every part of Zane, every point of contact from the wet heat encompassing his cock, to the hand that snaked up Dante's chest felt like love.

Zane took half of Dante's cock in his mouth and sucked. The world went white, and Dante babbled frantically.

"Gonna come. Fuck, Zane. Shit."

Zane didn't move. His fingers dug into Dante's rib cage as Dante arched off the bed. He thrust his hips, pumping to the motion of his cock twitching, and emptying in Zane's mouth.

Dante panted as the room spun. Without breath or bones, Dante managed to communicate with Zane.

"Get up here."

Zane complied. He wiped the corner of his mouth with the back of his hand. He cocked a crooked grin at Dante. "That could take some getting used to." He hovered near Dante's mouth. "Can I kiss you?"

"You better."

Zane sealed his mouth over Dante's and all at once it was like he hadn't come at all. His cock twitched and stirred to life. He tasted himself on Zane's tongue. Tangy and not unpleasant.

Zane kissed the corner of Dante's mouth, then pressed their foreheads together. "We should go."

Dante wound his arms around Zane's neck. "What about you?" Dante wanted to put Zane in his mouth. He wanted to taste him, to feel his hardness against his tongue.

"What if the realtor shows up with some nice old couple who want to see the house and they walk in here and catch us with our dicks out?"

Dante's face flushed at the thought. That was definitely not an adventure Dante wanted to have. "Point taken." Dante tucked his dick back in his pants and zipped up. He lay on his bed and stared at the ceiling, then Zane. "It's weird to know I'm not coming back here."

"Will you miss it?"

Dante shook his head. "I slept here. I ate here. I did homework here, but I don't think I ever lived here."

"Then let's get out of here." Zane stood and held his hand out for Dante to take.

Zane pulled Dante to his feet and into his arms. He kissed Dante's forehead. "You okay?"

Dante nodded, but he wasn't sure. "I'm okay with us. It's everything else." Dante sighed. He didn't have the words to articulate how he felt. On one hand, he was deliriously happy. Having Zane back, knowing he was sorry, he missed Dante, and he wanted to be with him, it was everything. It should have been enough to wipe out the dark, lost feeling that swelled up inside him.

He shouldn't have expected anything different from his mom, but he'd tried so hard over the years to be unobtrusive in her life. He didn't like to make waves, thinking that the less of an inconvenience he was, the more she'd want to have something to do with him, because he wasn't work. But all it had done was teach her that she could disappear.

Zane kissed his temple. "Let's get out of here." He stacked two boxes on top of each other and carried them to the bedroom door. "Anything else you want?"

Dante shook his head.

He rode back to Zane's without speaking. He felt... homeless. He knew his mother loved him in her own way, but not the way a mother should love their son. She loved him like a third favorite sports team. She knew he existed. When she remembered that fact, she might even like him, but most of the time, he didn't ping her radar as being important enough to think of.

Dante hadn't noticed how close they were to Zane's house until the car stopped. Dante looked up and blinked.

"You look tired. Why don't you go lay down in my room and I'll pack all this stuff inside?" Dante nodded and went to unbuckle his seatbelt. Zane leaned in and kissed him. "Did you want me to lay down with you?"

"Your parents—"

"Know I'm bisexual."

This whole day had been a rollercoaster of upswings and violent downs. Dante had Zane back, his parents knew he was bi. Both of those were good things. But Zane was still coming to the end of his college life, and Dante wasn't sure he had a home anymore beyond his tiny shared dorm room. Dante had never felt so temporary before, like he was as disposable as a napkin.

"Could I... would you be upset if I hung in Jonathan's room for a while. Alone?" Dante worried his lip between his teeth. He just got Zane back, and he didn't think Zane was the sort of fragile flower who needed constant reassurance from his boyfriend.

"It's fine. I promise. You go up, I'll get this stuff into the garage for now, okay."

"Thank you."

Dante slipped into the house and managed to avoid running into Zane's parents. They were in the kitchen when he arrived and though they called out a greeting, he pretended not to hear, and slid into Jonathan's bedroom.

Jonathan's bedroom always fascinated Dante. The arrangement of art on his walls was always changing. It wasn't organized. Papers of different weights and textures covered the walls. Some were sketches. Some were watercolor. He'd gone through a pastel phase not long before the end of high school and had done a series of disjointed landscapes.

Dante flopped down on Jonathan's bed and stared at them. The old fear that he'd lose all this came back. Jonathan was all he had left. Jonathan and Zane and Claire and Tony and this house that felt more like home than the house he grew up in.

Dante's phone chimed and he pulled it out of his pocket. Of course, it was Jonathan. Dante answered the video call. "Hey, look where I am." Dante panned the phone around.

"I thought you'd be there by now." Jonathan's gaze flickered down. "Is that a hickey?"

Dante's eyes widened. "Uh..."

"Guess you and the mystery man got back together."

Dante's face turned the color of a tomato. "Yeah."

"Why do you look fucking miserable then? It's Thanksgiving. You're home. You get to hang with the family and eat mom's pie. What's there to be upset about?"

"Mom's selling the house."

"Your mom? When? What? Isn't she in Kentucky?"

"Yeah."

"Did she send you a shitty text?"

Dante almost laughed at how absurd it was. "I found out today when I went there to get a few things I left behind in the fall. There's a for sale sign in the front yard."

"That's fucking cold. Jesus fucking christ. What is *wrong* with her?"

Jonathan's rage made Dante happy in a twisted way. It validated the things he felt in his heart. He used to try to make excuses for her, but when it came down to it. She wasn't a good mother. She was barely a mother at all. Not like Claire. Claire, who loved her children. Who did things like pick them up in the middle of the night from a party to make sure they got home safe.

"Can we not talk about this anymore?" Dante asked. "Tell me about the exhibit. Or your current projects or the beaches or something. Have you checked out Hollywood yet?"

"Sure did." Jonathan launched into a thirty-minute story about getting lost looking for the walk of fame and ending up on the other side of Los Angeles. Dante was sure half of it was bullshit. Jonathan was far too smart to be so stupid, but he appreciated his friend's effort to keep his mind off his trash pile home life.

By the time the call ended, Dante was exhausted. He didn't even realize he'd fallen asleep until he woke to Zane crawling into the bed next to him. Dante rolled into his arms and buried his face in Zane's chest.

"How are you doing?" Zane whispered.

"I'm okay. Hungry." Dante's stomach rumbled and Zane chuckled softly.

"Dinner's ready. Come on down. Mom made lasagna."

"Cafeteria food is going to suck when we go back. Lasagna tonight. Turkey tomorrow. All the pies."

"I'll convince mom to send a couple pies back with us."

Dante tilted his head back and kissed Zane's chin. "My hero."

CHAPTER 25

ZANE

Anger choked Zane but he bit it back and painted on what he hoped was a neutral expression. His parents sat at the kitchen table, each with a cup of coffee. Zane made a beeline for the fridge and grabbed a soda, though what he wanted was the burn of whiskey. Zane had never entertained the idea of hitting a woman before, but the thought of Dante's mom and her latest brand of bullshit had Zane on the ragged edge. He was lucky she was in Kentucky and hadn't been home when they showed up or Zane might have lost it.

"You okay, son?" Zane's dad asked.

"Dante's mom is selling the house, which he found out when we pulled up and saw the for-sale sign in the yard."

Zane's mom cursed under her breath. She wasn't the type of person who enjoyed being mean to or about people, but often he watched her struggle with the way Dante was treated.

"That... woman," she snarled, gripping her coffee mug. "She better move far away or I swear I'll cut her if I see her. Is Dante okay?"

"He's upset. He's up in Jonathan's room."

"I should go talk to him." Zane's mom started to stand.

"I think he wants to be alone for a while."

After a brief hesitation she sighed and sat. "Fine. But I reserve the right to check on him if he's up there too long."

Zane wanted to take Dante's mind off everything, and he had the perfect idea, but it required leaving for a while, which he was hesitant to do. But he thought Dante might appreciate the distraction. He finished his soda and tossed the empty can into the recycle bin under the sink.

"I have an errand to run, do you guys need anything while I'm out?"

"Get me a dozen eggs and a super pack of toilet paper."

"Claire," Zane's dad leveled her a look, even though the corner of his mouth quirked up.

"Fine. Never mind. I'll wait for Karma to take the bitch out."

Zane wished Dante had a better mom, one like his who loved her kids and didn't care who knew it. One who would always put him first.

He couldn't change things for Dante, but he could make them better. Zane's stomach flip-flopped all the way to the pharmacy. He was negative, his test results had been fine, and Dante hadn't been with anyone besides him, but safe was good. Zane bought a box of condoms and a couple of small, easily hidden bottles of lube.

He tossed his purchases on the passenger seat and instead of going home, Zane sat in the parking lot outside the pharmacy and called Ricky. He wanted to be ready for anything Dante wanted. If Dante wanted to top, or bottom, Zane wanted to be able to make it good for him, but he'd never done it before, and nerves crawled up his spine. The voice in his head had him half convinced that he'd murder Dante with his dick if he stuck it in that tiny, pretty hole of his.

"Hey man, what's up?" Ricky answered. In the background, Zane heard low music and quiet laughter.

"Shit, you're busy."

"Only a little. What do you need?"

Zane was thankful that he was having this conversation over the phone and not in person.

"I'm back with Dante."

"Hallelujah, you do have a brain. I'm happy for you." Ricky whispered something to someone in the background. Whoever he was with made a happy sound.

"Thanks." Zane took a deep breath. "I want to—" god, he couldn't even say it. How pathetic was he? "I don't want to hurt him."

"So, don't break up with him again. Problem solved." Zane could hear the eye roll in Ricky's tone of voice.

"No. I want to have sex with him and hurting him is the last thing I want to do, so you need to help me out. Please."

Silence. Soul crushing, mortifying, silence. "Okay, fam. I got you. You need lube. Lots. Be generous. The more the better. There's no such thing as too much. Start with a finger, watch his face for reactions. His body will teach you what it likes, pay attention."

Zane could do that. He was good at paying attention to Dante. "Okay. What next?"

"Another finger. Have him bear down. Taking deep breaths also helps relax the muscles. If you want to rock his world, eat his ass," Ricky laughed.

"One finger. Two. Deep breaths. Lots of lube. Okay. I think I can do this."

"Yeah, you can. You could've googled this shit you know."

"What would I google? Anal for formerly straight dummies?"

"Exactly. And wear a condom."

"Yes, Dad."

"That's daddy, to you, sport."

"Shut the fuck up."

"That's a brilliant idea." Ricky's voice deepened and Zane knew the call was over before the line went dead. Zane didn't know who Ricky was wrapped up in, but he had his suspicions.

Zane tried not to think too much about what he planned for him and Dante. He couldn't let it cross his mind without getting hard and he still had an entire evening with his parents to get through.

His stupid dick stayed half-hard though, despite his best efforts. By the time he returned home, Dante was still upstairs, and Zane couldn't stay away any longer. He headed for the stairs but was intercepted by his mom.

"Oh. You're home. I was just going to go up and get Dante for dinner."

"I'll get him."

"It's lasagna tonight."

Zane grinned. "I love you."

"You love my food," she said, smiling at him, but motioning for him to move along. "Dinner will be ready in five minutes."

Zane entered Jonathan's room and found Dante asleep on the bed. He looked small and alone on the queen size mattress. Zane quietly closed the door and crawled into bed next to him.

He rolled into Zane's arms, warm and sleepy and snuggled into Zane's chest. He could've stayed there forever, but dinner waited. Besides food, Zane thought being around people who genuinely gave a shit about him might help Dante's mood.

With a little prodding, and the promise of pie, Dante got out of bed. He pressed his mouth against Zane's. The kiss was chaste and sweet, and it got Zane's motor running all over again. He wanted to pin Dante to the mattress and grind against him, kiss him senseless, and spend the rest of the night worshipping him.

"I have to take a piss. I'll be down in a minute." Dante kissed him again, then left the room and entered the bathroom across the hall.

Zane went downstairs and washed his hands in the kitchen sink then helped set the table. They were all just sitting down when Dante walked into the room.

"You look like you rested," Zane's mom rose and cut a slice of lasagna and served Dante first.

"He looks like he was attacked by a vacuum." Zane's dad laughed and the room stilled.

Zane's mom looked at the bright red and purple splotch of color on Dante's neck. Then she looked at Dante, then at Zane. Then at Dante. Then she looked at Zane's dad.

"I told you Dante and Jonathan would never go out."

Dante and Zane shared a look of absolute shock. But Dante didn't run, which Zane counted as a win. He reached over and tangled his fingers with Dante's.

Dante looked like a deer trapped in the headlights.

"So you did." Zane's dad dished himself a serving of salad and passed the bowl to Dante. "Salad? There's extra croutons."

Dante blinked. "I like croutons," he said, releasing Zane's hand to take the salad.

Zane's dad grabbed a piece of garlic toast and set it on his plate. His mom served him a slice of lasagna. "I'd welcome you to the family, kid, but you've always been family." Then his dad took a drink of his water like he hadn't just said the most perfect thing to the most important person in Zane's life.

"I uh…" Dante cleared his throat. "Thanks." He lowered his gaze and started in on his food. Dante lifted his head a minute later, his cheeks had turned the color of ripe tomatoes. "I'd like to tell Jonathan, if that's okay with everyone."

Zane nodded. He'd give Dante whatever he wanted.

The dinner was absurdly normal after that. There were no questions about how they got together, or how long they'd been seeing each other. The lack of the third degree almost unsettled Zane, but it comforted him, too. The pink still hadn't faded from Dante's cheeks and he'd spent more time moving the food around his plate than he did eating it. He'd been through a lot all in one day and Zane was grateful he had parents who didn't suck. He knew he was lucky to have them, but most of the time he forgot. He tried not to take them for granted, but he made up his mind that going forward, he'd try a lot harder.

"Anyone want dessert?" Zane's mom asked as they all cleared the table.

"Maybe later," Dante said quietly.

Zane's mom sighed and reached for Dante. "Come here." Dante went, but instead of pulling him into a hug, she wrapped one arm over his shoulder. "Tony and I have a confession to make."

Zane watched Dante stiffen.

"We saw the for-sale sign on your house a couple weeks ago. We were upset, and we didn't know that you didn't know. We honestly thought you knew but hadn't told anyone. Well, anyway." She started walking down the hallway, toward the back of the house. They stopped outside a room which had been a craft room once upon a time. Then it had been a dance studio during Jonathan's *I want to be a dancer* stage. The door opened and the room had once again been transformed. A brand-new double bed. A dresser. The walls were freshly painted a grey-blue that matched Dante's eyes.

"What's this?" Dante's voice wavered.

"Your room. No matter what, you'll always have a home with us." The tremor in his mom's voice matched the one in Dante's. If they weren't careful, they'd have everyone crying.

"What if Zane and I don't work? What if he hates me? What if Jonathan hates me?" Dante babbled, but Zane's mom remained unfazed. She pulled Dante into her arms and hugged him tight.

"It doesn't matter. You're ours. You've always fit in here. I've thought of you as one of my boys for as long as I've known you. You will always have a home here."

Zane's dad cleared his throat and left the room. Dante looked worried at his departure, but Zane smiled at him. "Dad doesn't like to cry in front of the kids."

Dante's watery laugh turned into a sob and he wrapped his arms around Zane's mom and squeezed his eyes shut.

Zane took a step toward his boyfriend, but his mom made eye contact. "Can you give us a few minutes, sweetheart?"

"Dante?"

Dante sniffled and nodded. "It's okay. I'm..." he cleared his throat and pulled away, wiping at his eyes. "I'm okay."

"We'll be right out."

Zane stole a kiss and left Dante in the very capable and loving hands of his mother. He went to the kitchen and pulled two beers from the fridge. He cracked them both open and carried one out to his dad.

He passed his dad a beer and they drank quietly for a few minutes. "It's fucking cold out here." His dad shivered and took another sip.

"Then why are we out here?"

"Do you think they're done talking yet?"

Zane laughed. "It's fine. They're in Dante's room. You're not going to get any more feelings all over you."

"I love the kid like my own, Zane, so if you hurt him..." The warning came without any real malice or bite. His dad was a giant puppy who couldn't hurt a fly. "If you hurt him, I'll sic your mother on you."

Zane grimaced. "I don't plan on hurting him." Zane patted his dad on the shoulder. It should have been insulting to have his parents stick up for Dante, to protect him from any perceived threat to his happiness, but it made Zane smile bigger and brighter.

CHAPTER 26

DANTE

"Sit with me," Claire said. Dante sniffled and did as he was told, grabbing a space on the edge of the bed next to her. Claire wrapped an arm around him and tugged him close. She'd done it a thousand times over the course of his life. "You've had quite the day."

Dante nodded and glanced around the room. Claire and Tony had gone the extra mile for him, without knowing he was with Zane. His acceptance into their family had no bearing on his relationship with their oldest son.

"I don't know what to say," Dante's voice cracked, and new tears threatened to fall. God, he was sick of crying, but this day had been all over the map.

"You don't have to say anything." Claire paused and took a deep breath. "When Tony told me about the sign, his first thought was that we'd never see you again. That your mom would leave the city, and you'd go visit her and you'd never come back here. Maybe once in a while when Jonathan dragged you home. And we decided we wanted you to have a place here, so you knew, no matter what happens with your mom. No matter what happens with college or life or anything, you will always, always have a place here, Dante."

"Did you mean it when you said that you've always thought of me as yours?"

Claire turned to him and she smiled softly, sadly. "Yes, I did, Dante. I love you like you were my own."

Dante broke. He buried his face in his hands and let Claire tug him into a hug and he cried in the arms of the only real mother he'd ever known. Claire ran her fingers through his hair, soothing him with gentle hushes.

"This is your home, Dante. We're your family. Maybe we should've made it clear sooner."

Dante laughed. It was thick and watery, but it bubbled out of him. "I'm sort of glad you didn't because if I'd ever thought of Zane as a brother, dating him would have been super awkward."

Claire's laugh joined his and she kissed him on the cheek. "We should go out there if you're ready. The boys are probably getting worried."

"One thing first." Dante swallowed a bundle of nerves. "Can I call you Mom?"

Claire beamed. "You precious child. Of course, you can. And don't tell the others, but you're my favorite."

Dante grinned, broad and smug. "Oh, we already know that."

"Smartass." Claire stood and tugged Dante to his feet.

They found Tony and Zane in the kitchen, each of them had a beer in their hand. Tony ruffled Dante's hair as he passed.

Claire slid her arm through Tony's. "Do we need to have the safe sex talk?"

"Mom!" Zane blushed. "We have it under control, I promise."

"Yeah, dear, we raised responsible kids. And it's not like they can get pregnant."

"Really, Tony?" Claire rolled her eyes. "That's your contribution to this conversation?"

"What?" He smiled at her. "It's true, isn't it?"

Claire patted his bicep. "You're fired."

Dante squirmed, mortified by the direction the conversation had gone.

"You're scaring them," Tony pulled Claire into his arms and tugged her away from Zane and Dante.

"I am not," she said through her laughter. "I'm being a responsible parent. I want them to be safe."

"They'll never have sex if you keep talking to them about it."

Zane, thankfully, pulled Dante out of the room and up the stairs. They didn't speak until they'd escaped into Zane's room and shut the door.

"Oh my god. I can't." Zane pulled Dante into his arms and buried his face into the crook of Dante's neck. "Can you believe them?"

Dante didn't answer. He crushed himself close to Zane and shut his eyes. As happy as he felt in that moment, the day had been a total soap opera and he mostly wanted it over with.

"You okay?"

"Tired," Dante mumbled. "Long day."

"The longest," Zane agreed. Zane untangled himself from Dante long enough to stretch out on the bed and take Dante with him. "I want to tell you a couple things. Nothing bad."

Dante sighed and rested his head on Zane's chest. "Good, because my brain is getting ready to turn off for the day. Or the week. I can't do another bad."

"I got tested."

Zane's blurted confession made Dante lift his head and look Zane in the eyes. "When?"

"When we were apart. When I decided I needed to get you back. I didn't want to come back to you empty handed. I have a job lined up for after college. We can live together if you want. You can go to school and I'll support you."

Dante kissed Zane's chin. "I didn't need any of that. I only needed you."

"I know, but I was stupid."

"No one's perfect."

"You're pretty close."

"Flattery will get you everywhere." Dante bit his lip. His voice, when he finally found it again, was but a whisper. "You got tested?"

Zane dragged his hand down Dante's back and to his ass. "I did. I also bought lube and condoms. I know most people want things to be spontaneous, but I wanted you to know ahead of time; when you're ready, so am I."

Dante's blood heated. He was suddenly too fully dressed for his state of arousal. At the mere mention of sex, Dante was ready to strip naked and spread himself wide and invite Zane inside. Taking Zane appealed to him, and maybe he'd try that another time, but for now, he wanted that fullness people talked about. He wanted to experience connection with someone. With Zane.

"Please." Dante's fingers brushed Zane's bare throat. "Don't make me wait."

"My parents are downstairs." Zane said, even as he rolled over on top of Dante.

"I'll be quiet. So quiet."

"What if I want to hear all your sweet little sounds?"

Dante sighed. "Not fair."

"They always hit up the black Friday sales. We have to wait a little longer and we'll have the whole house to ourselves and you can be as noisy as you want."

"You mean I can be as noisy as *you* want."

"Something like that."

Dante was about to make an overture about how he didn't need his first time to be special, but maybe Zane did. Maybe Zane wanted candles, or roses, or at least a day that hadn't been a total shit fest.

"Forget about them. There is no them." Zane kissed the corner of Dante's mouth. "Shower with me."

"Yeah." Dante sighed. As eager as he was to do this, to experience all of Zane, he wanted to wash this day off his skin. He was okay now. For a few horrible minutes during the day, Dante had been falling. Falling hard and fast. Crashing as his world dropped out from underneath him. But Zane had been there to pull the ripcord.

They slipped into the bathroom without talking. The anticipation between them hung in the air, thick and heady. They stepped under the spray and they went about washing, taking turns moving out from under the spray so the other person could rinse and wash. Their touches were brief, but far from casual. Even the simple act of Zane's hand on Dante's hip, guiding him as they danced around each other to change positions, was erotic.

It wasn't a touch. It was a promise. It felt like one. Like Zane vowing to worship Dante's body, to cherish him. Dante rinsed the last of the soap from his chest and looked at Zane over his shoulder. He was incredibly sexy. It was hard for Dante to believe Zane liked him. That out of all the people in the universe who Zane could have, it was Dante he wanted.

And then Zane smiled at him, and his eyes danced with lust and a fondness, a softness Dante hadn't seen in his expression before, and he knew he'd put it there. Dante killed the spray and shook the water from his hair.

They toweled off in the small upstairs bathroom, nearly

bumping into each other in the process. They wrapped towels around their waists and Dante collected their clothing up off the floor.

"And that's why you're the favorite." Zane rolled his eyes, but his jab was good-natured.

"It's called not being a heathen. You should try it some time." Dante followed Zane into his bedroom and dropped the clothing, and his towel, in a heap in the middle of the floor. He gave it a kick for good measure. "Is that better?"

Zane tossed his towel aside then scooped him up and tossed him on the bed. Dante bounced, his limbs flailed, and he laughed as Zane lunged for him.

"I always wanted to do that." He crawled up Dante's body, covered him with his. Bare skin all the way down, naked like he'd never been, but not because he wasn't wearing clothes. Dante was naked all the way through. He trembled with want. With happiness. With hope. With a thousand other things fluttering in his insides like fireflies. Delicate like butterflies, but brighter. Warmer. Something that lit up the darkness. Something that made him feel safe, even in this most vulnerable moment.

Dante smoothed his hands across Zane's chest. He followed the line of his collarbone. He grazed his fingers over the taut muscles in Zane's shoulders. And a split second before all his courage went out the window, Dante opened his mouth and made himself speak the words that had lived in the back of his mouth for too long now. Words he'd been afraid of, because loving things was dangerous, but loving Zane wasn't. It was safe. Right.

"I love you." Dante didn't blurt it like he thought he would. It came out soft, like a secret between them, something delicate.

Zane's mouth descended on his and he teased a soft, tantalizing kiss from Dante's lips. He poked his tongue inside Dante's mouth and sank down on top of him, blanketing him in his warmth.

Zane kissed him dizzy. His body thrummed and pulsed. He wanted more. More more more more more. But he was content to let this moment stretch out and make everything else around them grey out.

Zane pulled away, depriving Dante of his sweet taste. He felt a puff of air against his lips.

"I love you, too."

Dante had been wrong before. He hadn't known what happiness was. And maybe it was a dangerous thing, to let his joy hinge on the words of another person, but for now, Dante would relish this feeling. This light, floaty, endlessly perfect moment.

CHAPTER 27

ZANE

Before Dante, Zane hadn't realized that men could be beautiful. But beneath him lay an angel with kiss-swollen lips and dark eyelashes that fanned over his cheeks before they fluttered open again. Shimmering blue eyes looked up at him and Zane's heart did laps in his chest.

Zane had loved before. But not like this. Loving Dante felt bigger and more real, more right than anything he'd ever felt. He kissed his love again. He was gentle, but insistent. He needed Dante in a way he'd never needed anyone, and it made him nervous. God, he was afraid. Afraid of hurting Dante, or of not making him feel good. Afraid of fucking things up again.

"You think too much." Dante whispered, though the house was empty. It was a moment for quiet words between lovers and Zane closed his eyes. He let the silence between them wrap around him like an embrace. It soothed him, the stillness of everything, like the world had paused to let them have this.

Desire burned through him and he lowered himself down on top of Dante, lined up their bodies, and with a wicked grin, he undulated his hips. Dante's mouth fell open and he let out a little gasp. Zane kissed him, unable to stop himself. Dante appeared delicate and delicious, like a dessert Zane still couldn't believe he got to consume.

Dante sighed into his mouth. Whimpered when Zane repeated the motion with his hips.

"I want you so bad," Zane confessed. Beneath him, Dante's hips rose to meet his.

"Please."

Excitement. Nerves. Ecstasy. Happiness. A thousand things flooded Zane's brain and he thought he might short circuit.

"Tell me what you want. I'll give you anything. Anything at all. I'm yours."

Dante's lips found his and they were kissing again. Desperate and hungry, they were on fire. Their bodies seemed to move of their own accord, seeking pleasure and satisfaction. Nothing had ever felt so good.

"You," Dante panted when he pulled away. "You, in me."

Zane's cock twitched. "We can do it the other way if you want. I don't expect you to bottom."

Dante smiled. Sweet and shy and just for him. "I know what I want."

Zane took a deep breath. "Okay."

Before they went any further, he leaned over and dug in his nightstand where he'd stashed the condoms and the lube. He tossed them out of the way, but in reach and claimed Dante's mouth again.

Dante kissed with his entire body. Their lips and tongues danced together, in a wet erotic slide into lust, but Dante's hand touched Zane everywhere. His hair. Shoulders. Neck. Back. His hips came up, chased Zane's, his legs spread wider, allowing Zane to sink between them. He gave Zane all of himself.

Zane kissed his way down Dante's chest. He relished the expanse of smooth skin, the undefined stomach, and the slightly bony hips. He nestled his nose in against the base of Dante's cock. He laughed when Dante trembled.

"I want to taste you," Zane made to wrap a hand around Dante's cock.

"I'll come. I'm already almost there. I don't want to come yet."

Zane kissed the crease of Dante's thigh instead and reached for the lube. "Spread your legs wider for me, okay, baby."

Legs spread to the sound of a breathy laugh and Dante planted his feet on the mattress, which gave Zane better access. He coated his fingers with lube and teased them into Dante's crease.

His other hand slid up Dante's chest. Zane meant to toy with him, to touch him, distract him from his fingers circling his rim, dancing on the edge, spreading lube around and preparing him for penetration. Dante grabbed his hand. He grabbed his hand and twined their fingers together and squeezed.

Zane lifted his head and pressed the tip of his finger inside Dante. "Deep breaths," Zane coached. "Try to relax."

Dante laughed a little. "I've put fingers in my ass before, Zane." To prove his point, Dante did some sort of magic with his muscles and they loosened, allowing Zane to slide his finger in.

It was warm and tight, soft, but holy shit, he couldn't imagine getting another finger in there, let alone his cock.

Dante panted and squirmed. "Move. Please."

Zane slowly withdrew the finger, then pushed it back in. He built a rhythm, slow and unsure at first, but watching his finger slip into Dante was the hottest thing he'd ever done, and he wanted to imprint it into his memory. Every breath and twitch.

Zane slid in a second finger and Dante moaned. His fingers flexed, gripping Zane's hand tighter.

"You good?" Zane asked, flicking his gaze up to Dante's face.

His eyes were shut, and he had his bottom lip pinched in his teeth.

Dante nodded. "So good."

Zane's cock throbbed with the need to fuck Dante. He pressed another kiss to the crease of Dante's thigh. Precum oozed from Dante's cock, which had briefly flagged during the first few minutes of penetration, but was now at full mast, hard and leaking against his stomach.

He fingered him until he was loose and slick. Until his chest was red with lust and his breathing came in erratic pants. Until Dante shook and begged for more.

Zane carefully drew his fingers out of Dante, untangled their fingers and rocked back on his heels. He rolled a condom down his cock and added lube. Then, remembering Ricky's words of wisdom, he added a bit more. He slid his hand down his cock and he stared at Dante.

His insides trembled like gelatin during an earthquake, but he moved in with a confidence he didn't feel. Dante lifted his legs and draped them over Zane's. Zane nestled in close and lined his cock up with Dante's hole. And pressed forward.

"Lower," Dante panted, his hips rising to try and line Zane up better. Zane pressed forward again, but his cock slipped out of position.

Dante laughed. His hands found Zane's knees. "It's okay. Try again. I'm ready. You won't hurt me."

Zane took a deep breath and tried again. The tip breached Dante and Zane sucked in a deep breath before pressing in further. Dante's brow furrowed and one hand wrapped around his cock. Zane's thighs trembled as he pressed in slowly.

"Fuck you're tight."

Dante giggled, his already flushed face turned crimson. "Virgin, remember?"

Zane tried to laugh, but couldn't, because he inched in further and it stole his breath. The tight heat. The way Dante's muscles moved when he laughed. The look on his face. Zane's balls pulled up tight to his body, hot and ready and waiting for release.

Zane leaned forward and pressed his open mouth to Dante's. He breathed him in and slid inside until Dante whimpered and panted and Zane couldn't push in any deeper. Then he breathed. In and out and desperately tried to get the rising tide of lust under control.

Dante writhed and rocked underneath him, his hand still wrapped tight around his cock. Dante whimpered and Zane moved. Slowly, as to not hurt Dante. Out. Then in. Dante's kiss trembled. Or maybe it was Zane. Dante clung to him, arms around his shoulders, one hand sunk into his hair, preventing Zane from stopping the kiss, as if he had the urge to stop doing anything at that precise moment.

Dante's hand moved between them, sliding over his cock, tugging, chasing his own release. Zane felt his orgasm build in his spine and he didn't stop kissing Dante to warn him. He kissed him harder, with a surety that this was the last person he'd ever kiss.

And then he came. He kept himself from slamming into Dante the way his body wanted to, but he came hard and long. He pumped and thrust, feeling Dante's muscles clamp around him as warm, sticky cum coated Dante's chest, Zane's chest, Zane's chin.

Zane laughed, and their kiss finally broke. He rested his forehead on Dante's.

"You okay? I didn't hurt you, did I?"

"You didn't hurt me. And I'm way more than okay."

Zane was loathe to pull out, but he couldn't imagine it was comfortable to have a dick in your ass after you'd already come (he made a mental note to experiment with Dante one day and see for himself).

He kept one hand on the base of his dick and eased out of Dante. He tossed the condom into the empty trash can near the bed and collapsed next to Dante. Dante rolled over and into Zane's arms. He laid his head on Zane's chest and snuggled close.

"I'm glad I didn't go with Linden this weekend."

"Oh, had an alternative offer, did you?" Zane kissed the top of Dante's head. He was glad Dante had a small group of friends of his own at college. Watching Dante come out of his shell these past few months had been amazing to see. He'd never be the outgoing type, but it was good to see him stretch his wings.

"Even tried to bribe me with the promise of a food coma."

"But you came with me anyway."

"Well, what can I say. I'm a sucker for punishment. I'd follow you anywhere. I'm sort of in love with you."

"Oh, only sort of?"

Dante laughed. "Sort of."

Zane rolled over on top of him and pinned him down. "That's not what you said earlier. Admit it. You're crazy about me. Over the moon. Can't eat, can't sleep, crazy about me."

Dante rolled his eyes. "Fine. Have it your way. I'm crazy about you. Over the moon." Dante wrapped his arms around Zane's neck and pulled him in for another kiss.

CHAPTER 28

DANTE

Dante sat down at the dining room table next to Zane. The food was laid out in the center. It was more than they could ever eat in one meal and it was more than Dante ever had with his mom, who had texted him early in the morning to wish him a happy thanksgiving. Dante replied that he'd moved the rest of the stuff he wanted out of his room and then turned his phone off.

Zane didn't press him about it, he held him and kissed him, and they didn't have sex again because Dante was sore. It was a pleasant ache, a barely there twinge, but they were content to just be with each other, whatever that meant in the moment. Whether it was cuddling naked in bed, whispering late into the night, or sitting around the table watching Zane's dad carve the turkey.

Dante heaped his plate with a little of everything. Mashed potatoes, gravy, turkey, brussels sprouts, which made Zane give him a sour look.

"You're brushing your teeth before you kiss me with your sprout mouth."

"Yes, dear."

"You two already sound like an old married couple."

Dante's head snapped around to see Jonathan standing in the entrance to the dining room. "Holy shit."

"Happy Thanksgiving to you, too." Jonathan grinned and hugged his mom, who jumped up from her seat.

"What are you doing home?" She asked. "You were staying for that exhibit."

"Yeah well, when the artist you planned to see is shuffled off to rehab after an overdose and the show is cancelled, it sort of... well... here I am. Surprise."

"Oh, baby. I'm sorry about the exhibit." Claire gave his arm a squeeze. "Why don't you sit, and I'll get you a plate."

"Good to have you home son." Tony looked pleased as punch to have all his boys home.

Jonathan turned his attention to Zane and Dante. "Am I the last to know? Like, officially know, I mean. I knew weeks ago that the two of you had a thing going on."

Dante opened his mouth. Closed it. Said nothing. Was Jonathan mad? He didn't look mad. He took his plate and silverware from his mom with a polite thank you, then dished himself up.

"Seriously, Dante, don't be so surprised. I didn't think Zane was anything but straight, but once the two of you started acting all lovey dovey on video calls and shit, and the fact you were never apart. Then you were always apart. I might not be a rocket scientist, but I can add two and two."

"I'm sorry," Dante croaked.

Jonathan seemed unfazed by his apology. In fact, he smiled. "I'm not. You get to be my brother forever now because I'm not letting you to break up. Ever. It would be too weird."

Zane reached over and ruffled Jonathan's hair. "Thanks for your approval. Not that it was needed."

Jonathan swatted Zane's hands away. "Don't touch the hair."

Zane might not have needed Jonathan's approval, but Dante did, and he hadn't known how badly until he had it. A weight lifted from his chest and he blinked back a tear. He didn't know what to say, so he picked up his fork and tucked into his dinner.

He hadn't lost anything and maybe he didn't have to. Maybe he could keep everything after all. Claire and Tony weren't like his mom. They had made room for him, they always had. Hell, they made *a* room for him. Dante wanted to put his things in there, even if he planned on staying with Zane in his room, he wanted some sort of permanence.

Dante cleared his throat and looked at Jonathan. "I uh... my stuff is in the garage, but Claire and Tony." Dante shifted his gaze. "Mom and Dad said I could put it in my room downstairs. Do you want to help after dinner?"

"Do you remember when I begged for the downstairs bedroom and they wouldn't give it to me?" Jonathan grinned.

"That's because you asked for it after you broke your arm falling off the roof trying to sneak out of the house. We weren't about to aid and abet your teenage rebellion." Claire said smoothly. "Now eat your vegetables."

Jonathan rolled his eyes. "Yeah, of course I'll help you, is all I was going to say."

Zane stayed back and helped his parents clean up after dinner while Dante and Jonathan carried his stuff from the garage into the room he now had, but probably would never use. Well, hopefully he'd never use it.

"When did you figure it out? Me and Zane, I mean." Dante asked. He flopped down on the bed and tucked his hands behind his head trying to appear more nonchalant than he felt.

"Pretty much right away, I think. You wouldn't tell me anything about the guy you were interested in, which meant one of two things." Jonathan flopped down next to him and mirrored his pose. They stared at the ceiling together. "It meant he was some sort of bad boy who I wouldn't approve of, or it was my dumbass brother. When he flung his arm around you on that one video chat though, that's when I knew. You guys were so fucking happy. It wouldn't have killed you to tell me, you know."

"I was scared," Dante could admit that now. "Sometimes I still am. This family is all I have. All I've ever had."

"You could divorce my brother ten times and I'd still love you to hell and back, Dante."

Dante didn't know what to say. The certainty in Jonathan's voice soothed him. Maybe he should've told Jonathan sooner. It might have eased his fears from the beginning if he'd been honest.

"We're family, Dante. And I know you have a fucked up idea of what that means because your mom is a fucking ghost, but in this house, it means we love you no matter what. Whether you fail a class or fall out of a window and bust your arm sneaking out of the house, or accidentally set the shed on fire. It's not conditional. Basically, you're fucking stuck with us."

"Rooftops are overrated." Dante laughed at Jonathan's puzzled expression. He'd have to tell him about setting the alarm off trying to get to the roof and the subsequent ankle ruining dash down the stairs. But it could wait. "There are worse people to be stuck with."

"Ditto, asshole."

Dante kicked Jonathan, a sharp jab to the shin. Jonathan retaliated almost immediately with a fierce snap of his foot against Dante's calf.

They laughed for a minute, then slid into a comfortable silence.

"I'm sorry I didn't tell you."

"It's fine. Like... it pissed me off a little to begin with, but I get it. Zane didn't even know he was into guys. I can see why you guys wanted to keep it private for a while. But I'm not losing my best friend to some asshat who shares my DNA or some college punk with a dumb name. You're going to not share the gross details, but I still want all the perks of being best friends. You're going to tell me when he pisses you off and I'm going to take your side, like I always would, and we're going to rant and bitch about him before you go kiss and make up."

"And we'll still do stuff. Just the two of us," Dante promised.

"Fun stuff, or shit like this where I help you move boxes around?"

"Zane and I have to leave the day after tomorrow, but we should do something tomorrow. There's that museum you always drag me to with the art I don't understand. Let's do that and after we can grab milkshakes."

"You're buying."

"Hey, I'm a broke ass college kid."

"Fine. Mom and Dad are buying." Jonathan laughed and kicked Dante's calf again, gently this time.

Jonathan and Dante hung out a little more before joining the rest of the family in the living room. Zane saved him a spot next to him on the love seat and Dante sat next to him, then curled into his side.

"You two are gross." Jonathan pretended to gag.

"What was that I heard?" Zane asked. "Did I hear you say you wanted an atomic wedgie?"

"Nope. I said absolutely nothing." Jonathan sat in the recliner and tilted himself back.

"That's what I thought." Zane wrapped his arm around Dante's shoulders.

Dante slipped into Zane's bed later that night and burrowed into his boyfriend's side.

"You're quiet," Zane whispered in the dark.

"I'm happy," Dante smiled and kissed Zane's bare chest. He never thought he'd be in his first year of college when he found his happily ever after. He never dreamed it would be Zane who turned his world upside down and filled it with joy and love and laughter, but it couldn't have worked out better had he planned it himself.

"Me too." Zane cupped Dante's cheek and tilted his head and kissed him. "Happiest man alive."

Dante didn't know what the future looked like. He knew whatever it was, Zane would be in it. And Jonathan. And parents who took him in as one of their own. It was more than he thought he'd ever have. It was more than enough. It was perfect.

The End

ABOUT THE AUTHOR

E. M. Denning is a married mom of three and a writer from British Columbia. Author of endearing filth and schmoopy sex, also addicted to books and coffee. She writes romance for the 18+ crowd.

Follow her on Facebook
Subscribe to her newsletter
Join her Facebook group Denning's Darlings

Future Fake Husband

Future Gay Boyfriend

Future Ex Enemy

With Kate Hawthorne and E.M. Lindsey

Cloudy with a Chance of Love